THE HAUNTED PAST OF BIRDIE

TALIA ATKINS

CONTENTS

Trigger Warnings

Like all my other books, I will list the possible triggers in this book. But please be advised, if dark thriller romances and graphic content is not your cup of tea then I recommend going no further then this... If you read trigger warnings like it's a menu then let me list the entrée, main and desert ;)

Abduction

Stalking

Dubcon

Violence

Incest (one scene)

TALIA ATKINS

Parental Death

Cult and brainwashing themes

Forced Medical Procedures

Self harm

Graphic sex scenes (including one MFM scene.)

Dedication

To my husband and kids for not taking it personally when I completely ignore all of you for my laptop. Me, diving into something other than mothering is new for us all.

Zoe, my editor, PA and biggest cheerleader. Thank you for being with me from the start, giving me encouraging words when I need them and having the same crazy sense of humor as me.

My readers, thank you for taking a chance on a new baby indie author like me.

There's something special about walking down a small-town street, the sun setting over the top of the surrounding mountains, hand-in-hand with the one you love. My eyes study the couple walking towards me. Her long, brown curls bounce against his shoulder, as she leans in and giggles against his broad shoulders, clothed in a soft flannel shirt. The plaid pattern teamed with faded jeans and lace-up work boots is a common theme with most guys in this town. I duck my head, sidestep the happy couple so we don't collide, and then look ahead once more. The long, narrow sidewalk in front of me is empty now, with the tall streetlights starting to slowly flicker to life, letting me know that the beautiful orange hue in the gray sky is about to become pitch black once more.

Coastal Town is, well, coastal and a town. *Go figure.* With a population of about two thousand citizens, it's tight-knit—so tight-knit that everyone knows everyone, and if you have anything going on in your personal life, they will all know about it. The township is situated along an oceanfront in northern America. It has large mountains along the inland side of town and an expansive ocean waterfront along the coast that sandwich a small network of shops and houses. It's remote, with one road in and one road out, but it means we are usually fairly safe from tourists and unwanted crowds of people.

I keep walking, snagging my backpack and pulling it tighter over my shoulder. My shift at the local coffee shop had been a long one, my throbbing feet a vibrant reminder. Nesting birds squawk loudly in nearby trees, protesting as I cross the road as if my proximity is an intrusion. My heavy breathing and burning lungs make me feel weak as my sneakers keep pounding the tarmac. As my small house comes into sight, I sigh with relief. Pushing open the small wooden gate that matches the timber fence around my small cottage, I burst up the cobbled footpath, tugging my house keys out of my back pocket as I near the front door. I fumble with the keys, and in haste, I miss the keyhole on the door a few times until it finally makes the click when it fits snugly in place. As I turn the key, a shiver runs up my spine. The feeling of being watched fills my senses, causing my arms to prickle with nervous goosebumps as I glance over my shoulder from instinct. After scanning the road and confirming all is clear, I push the door open and slam it shut firmly behind me. I lock it behind me before throwing my keys on the hallway shelves. My lips tug into a brief smile when my eyes brush over the photo of me and Mom, and I kick off my work sneakers and drop my backpack beside them. "Hey, Mom," I whisper in passing to the photo frame as I make my way straight to the shower. I don't need dinner tonight. I scoffed leftovers from the cafe cabinet that were going to get binned. I am always more than happy to eat what I can from the café because it saves on my food bill. Working in the local coffee shop is enough to cover my bills, but it doesn't leave money for much else. Although, in a town with nothing going on, you really don't need a lot of money to live here anyhow.

I make my way into the small bathroom that's off the one and only bedroom in this house. I turn the shower nozzle, filling the bathroom with the sound of the water pounding against the stainless-steel bottom, and then start stripping my clothes off. My reflection in the small, square mirror is a tired one. My fingertips lightly trace the deep purple bags under my blue eyes that stand out on my glowing summer-bronzed skin. Pulling my ponytail out, I grab fistfuls of my sandy-colored hair to reposition it into a top, messy bun so my long strands don't get wet in the shower. It's Monday today, which means I'm not due to wash my hair for another two days. Wednesday night and Saturday night are the nights I wash my hair. Keeping my life in a strict routine makes getting through each week just a little bit easier.

Stepping into the shower, I let the water fall over my body and soothe my aching feet. I wiggle my toes in the shallow water that's pooling at the bottom of the shower. It feels good to stretch them out, even though I know by midday tomorrow, they will feel exactly the same as they do today. As I lather soap suds over my arms and down my torso, I make a mental note that I need to order Mom's favorite flowers tonight so I know for certain they will be ready on Wednesday when I visit her for her birthday. Mom's favorite was always bright-colored gerberas. *They are bright and full of life like you should always be,* is what Mom has always told me. Five minutes later, I am tucked in my twin bed, sending through the flower order from my phone on the florist's website. Placing my phone on the bedside table and flicking my lamp off, I feel pleased with myself for getting another task out of the way. I smooth my floral bedspread over my body and lay my head back down into my duck-down pillow, enjoying the content feeling of everything being in order. But while I can control all aspects of my life the best I can while I am awake, when I am asleep, I am at the mercy of my nightmares.

I stare up at the ceiling, fear starting to grip me like a chokehold, lacing my fingers tightly together and resting my clasped hands on my stomach. My eyes focus on the fibers from the plasterboard underneath the old paint job. Ice-cold fear keeps my eyes glued to the same spot, hoping I can somehow stare all night long and skip the torment awaiting me. But no matter how hard I try, my eyes succumb to the blackness of deep sleep.

My lungs are tight. Heavy. I try to take a deep breath to relieve the pressure squeezing my lungs, but there is no air to take in. Gasps escape my mouth as I am on all fours, blanketed by complete darkness. It's like thick, black ink surrounding me at every turn. I lean back, resting on my knees, and scratch frantically at my throat. Hot tears stream down my cheeks and then onto my moving hands. Suddenly, my lungs inflate, and the tight hold around me seems to melt away along with the blackness. Trees appear all around, and the smell of fresh pine needles fills my senses. My head drops down, eyes focusing on my pained knees. My knees are bare, and blood coats them with twigs and gravel embedded deeply in my skin. I search my surroundings, desperately trying to find where I am and how to return to the safety of my bed. This isn't real, my mind screams. I stand slowly, squaring my shoulders with my fists balled at my sides. This isn't real! I burst out loudly at the top of my lungs. The sudden noise in the dense, quiet forest sends crows flying in every direction, soaring from the branches and foliage into the night sky. I watch them all scatter, leaving me staring up into the nothingness. An ice-cold breeze stirs around me, followed by a crunching of sticks behind me. I stand frozen in place, not daring to turn around. If I don't see it, if we don't make eye contact, then it doesn't exist. If I stay where I am, it will leave me alone. But I know better. My body starts shaking uncontrollably, teeth chattering painfully against each other so much you can hear them connecting. The monster in my nightmares never leaves me alone. It's here every time. "Come home," it says from behind me. The voice drips with evil. It promises torture and malice. "Leave me alone," I whisper back in a shaky voice. "You know you belong with us," it almost laughs at me tauntingly. Dried undergrowth crunches behind me, getting closer and closer to me. Dropping to the ground, I curl up into a fetal position, hugging my knees as tight as possible. This isn't real... This isn't real... This isn't real...

I wake with a jolt, sweat coating my entire body and drenching into the sheets beneath me. I gingerly lift my hand, placing it over my chest as if holding it there could slow down my hammering heart. Tilting my head towards the window, I realize it is morning when the light streams through my parted curtains. It doesn't feel like I have slept; in fact, I feel like I have been on a three-day bender, hitting every narcotic that I could have found. Sliding my legs over the side of the bed, I squint towards the light, hoping it will chase away the dread that seems to be following me around these days. In the last two weeks, this same nightmare has returned every single night. I get ready for work in a robotic way. My eyes feel dry and sting when I blink. I try not to look in the mirror. It won't do my self-esteem any good. I toss my hair into what should be a high ponytail, but the loose band makes it sag instantly, and flutters of hair hang loosely around my neck. I ignore it and get dressed.

I would like to say I graciously sauntered into work two hours later, but I didn't saunter anywhere. I stumbled my way in like a zombie in an apocalypse. My head is so numb and filled with the horrors from last night that when squeezing my feet into my canvas sneakers, I didn't even bat an eyelid. Physical pain had nothing on me today.

"Birdie, are you ill?" My boss and café owner, Sandy, asks me while wrapping her arm around my waist and pulling me against her. She is an older lady in her seventies and has always been touchy-feely. But not the bad kind. Like a mother or grandmother would be with her own family. "No, I'm just not sleeping very well at the moment, Sandy," I mumble, patting her hand on my hip while appreciating her warmth and nurturing touch.

"Are you going to see your Mom tomorrow?"

"Yep, of course. I have already ordered the flowers," I answer her and let her assume that my sleepless nights are from my mother's upcoming birthday. I don't need to tell Sandy about my nightmares because the truth is, if she asks me about them, I don't really know what I can say. I know what they are about, and they are recurring, but once I wake, they sort of become a blur, yet the horrific ice-cold fear is still deep in my core, making it impossible for me to forget that it had been a haunting nightmare.

"Alright, darling. Well, the apron's behind the counter, and if you need a time-out, just sing out, okay?"

"Okay," I smile at her, hoping it reaches my eyes and doesn't crack my tired face. Then I go grab my apron. As I tighten the apron strings around my hips, the small bell in the front glass door rattles, letting us know that a new customer has walked through the door. I push the stray strands of hair back towards my ponytail, clear my throat, and grab my notepad and pen. I glance to the door, watching a tall male figure walk between the tables, his head facing straight ahead. The stranger takes a seat in the far corner, dragging the seat out loudly as he gets comfortable. I make my way over to him, assessing the stranger's attire. He's new to town. And we don't ever get new. I know he is new because I know everyone in this small-ass town. He's also not dressed in your typical forestry worker or tradesman clothing. And he's most certainly not a fisherman. The customer is wearing black combat-style cargo pants and a dark gray tucked-in cotton shirt underneath a black leather jacket. He kicks a leg out, stretching wide, letting his physical form and energy around him dominate the space. I stop beside his table, clearing my throat once more, but I'm left viewing the top of his hair. He looks down towards the ground as if he's found something intriguing on the worn lino flooring. His hair is a similar color to mine, light sandy brown, but it has highlights through the straight, ear-length strands. I am tempted to ask him if they are natural or if he gets them done at a hairdresser. Instead, I chew on the inside of my cheek, hoping he will acknowledge me so I can take his order and scamper back to the front counter. I start tapping the tip of my sneaker on the floor, growing impatient.

"Coffee, please," his dark, commanding voice requests.

"Black or white?"

"Whatever you prefer," he says almost dismissively, but I catch a slight question in his tone.

"I prefer mine strong with extra cream," I chirp out, then, sucking in a breath, I stare at the ceiling, hoping it will swallow me whole. *I did not just say that.* The stranger's shoulders shudder slightly, flexing his firm leather jacket, giving me the impression he is amused by my answer. I turn on my heels and walk off through the small array of tables, feeling bemused by the new man in town. I am left wondering how long he will be here for. By the time I put the notepad on the order line, I realize my heavy thoughts of my night terrors are forgotten. I spent the next minute aimlessly rearranging the fresh flowers in the vase by the cash register while stealing glances at the far corner of the café. Still engrossed in the apparent wonderful, stained lino pattern, the man's head still hangs low. The summer light shines through the glass panes, the late-morning sun creeping in, making the stranger's hair look golden.

"Coffee's up for table ten kid," calls Toni from behind the coffee machine.

"Thanks, Toni," I say as I grab the large mug, smirking slightly when I see the extra cream on top. I carefully make my way to the back of the café and place the coffee mug down. He makes no effort to move, so I retreat to the front counter once more. *Well, he certainly isn't a people person.* He must just be stopping by and then leaving again. Taking extra care in the cleanliness of the counter, I spray it and wipe it down probably five times to stop myself from staring. While serving one of our regulars, the strange man walks up behind my customer and waits. I steal my eyes back to the lady in front of me, reminding myself not to be rude, although I am desperate to see what he finally looks like. I ring up the till, and taking the customer's cash, I put it in the till and awkwardly wait for the new stranger to pay for his coffee.

"How much do I owe you?" His deep voice echoes through the quiet space. I can feel eyes from every direction, trained on us both. Not because we are talking. But because of who I am talking to. A newbie. Our town is full of the curious kind who would want to know what this outsider wants.

"Five dollars, please," I answer, ignoring the stares around us. My eyes rake over his face, and what a face it is. He has a wide jawline and a sharp but not overly pointed nose. His eyes are a light chestnut brown with lighter flecks through it. His brows are thick, and his face holds a stern expression to it. Like smiling would give him an allergic reaction.

"Sure, here you go, ma'am."

"I think I am too young to be called ma'am," I humor him as I take the money. My hand skims his, and I can feel the hard calluses on his hands. Maybe he is a tradesman, after all. With hands like those, he definitely does some sort of manual work. "I guess you are right about that. What's your name?" he asks, yet the question seems more of a demand. I get the feeling he isn't told B*no'* very often.

"Birdie. You been in town for long? We don't get many newcomers stopping by."

"Nice name," he grunts but chooses not to answer my question. His brows furrow together as he turns toward the door to leave.

"Okay, Mr. Talkative," I mumble under my breath, but not quietly enough. He stops, angling himself slightly so he can see me over his shoulder. The corner of his lips twitch, forming a deep dimple in his cheek.

"Bye, Birdie," he grunts again and walks away, letting the bell in the doorway sing loudly at his exit.

"That was fucking weird."

"Birdie, do not cuss like that," Sandy says from behind me. But I could feel her eyes on the man who had just left and knew she agreed with my entire statement, cuss words and all. Toni comes round from the back of the kitchen where he rests his hands on the front counter where he watches the stranger retreat with Sandy and I.

"What do you think he wants, kid?"

"Not sure. He's not very talkative to say the least," I shrug. "Maybe he will carry on his way." Toni replies as he pushes himself back off the counter and heads back to his kitchen space.

Three hours later, I find myself walking along the sandy beach on the waterside. The café had been quiet, and Sandy said I looked like death on legs. I wasn't sure how I felt about that comment, but I had been told to head home for the day. Having come here straight from work, I am still in my black work shorts and deep purple T-shirt, the smell of the fried food and coffee beans I have become very much accustomed to deeply ingrained in the fabric. I sink down, drop my backpack, and slowly start pulling off my sneakers. I dig my toes into the warm, grainy sand before curling my fingers through it. This has been home to me and Mom since I was four years old. I have no other family. Mom never liked to speak of my father. She simply said I didn't have one and didn't need one. She always told me that her family lived far away and didn't get along. I never pressed Mom too much on the family issue. I could see how cut-up she became when we talked about it. I rest my chin on my knees while hugging my legs firmly.

Now I have turned twenty-one, I feel an emptiness in me. I feel lonely. Don't get me wrong, the whole Coastal Town treats me like I am their family. We are like a massive family. But I have no idea if I have any siblings, whether my father is alive, if he knows about me, or if I have grandparents who miss me. My childhood years at school had its challenges. When we did family history studies, cultural studies, and family sharing assemblies, I would be the loser with blank posters or sitting at the back with no family cultural heirlooms to share. Glancing over at the fishermen surfcasting off the beach, I decide it's time to head home. Maybe I could stop at the pharmacy and get some sleeping pills for tonight. I haven't tried any yet, but I need sleep, and the thought of sleep petrifies me. I unfold myself, stretching my arms high above my head as I stand. The jaw-cracking yawn that escapes almost hurts my face, and my eyes prickle with unshed tears. I pick up my belongings and turn, heading back towards the stairs that lead up to the main road. I watch my bare, sand-covered feet creep up the timber steps from the beach. The salty fresh air whipping around me and the crashing waves growing more distant distract me enough that I don't see the 6-foot giant in front of me, clad head to toe in black leather.

"Ah," I jump, dropping my bag harshly on the concrete footpath.

"I can see why you love it here," he says as he leans down to pick up my bag. The stranger from the café, straightens up and holds my bag out to me with a slight smirk. His eyes are soft and kind, a stark contrast from earlier.

"Ah, thanks," I say tentatively, taking the bag from his grasp. He drops his hand to the side, then tilts his head slightly as if trying to study me just as much as I am trying to subtly study him. "Where ya headed?" he asks, stuffing his hands in his jacket pockets.

"Drugstore," I admit quietly, then try to step around him. The glint of the black Harley behind him catches my eye, and then I study over his clothing again.

"This bike yours?"

"Yeah, best way to travel," he says, confirming my suspicions.

"I prefer two feet on the ground, but I will take your word for it."

He openly chuckles and shrugs his hefty shoulders.

"You are in a better mood compared to this morning." He gazes at me while his lips part as if to say something. Shaking his head softly as if deciding against what is on the tip of his tongue he changes the subject.

"So, why are you going to the drugstore?" I blanch at his prying question, making him put his hands up in defense. "Sorry, didn't mean to pry."

"You haven't even told me your name. At least I was polite and gave you mine."

"Sorry, Birdie. The name is Axel."

"Okay, well, nice to meet you again, Axel. I need to go now."

"Do you need a ride?" I stop short and stare at the midnight black bike in front of me, then turn slightly so I am angled to face Axel.

"I don't think so. But thanks." I turn to keep walking. I don't peek back—although curious and tempted—and keep my head pointed ahead. I need drugs, I need sleep, and I need to focus on Mom's birthday tomorrow. I have enough going on in my life without worrying about a tall man, covered head-to-toe in leather, giving me his mood swings. I walk two streets over, still barefoot, because, in a town like this, no one gives a crap. I could be walking around in a bikini or pajamas, and no one would bat an eyelid. Relaxed doesn't even begin to explain how we all live in this town.

I step into the drug store and head to the counter, greeting Fran as I near.

"Hi, Fran!" "Birdie! How's it going?" she says in a rush, our words almost overlapping. This is how Fran always speaks. She speaks quickly and usually speaks before thinking, too. At any town event, Fran will be the one to get herself in some sort of hot water for saying the wrong thing.

"Good, I'm not really sleeping at the moment. Is it possible to have some sleeping pills?" "Hmmm yeah, I can give you some light sleeping pills, or more of the natural kind, but I can't give you anything too strong without a doctor's prescription."

"Of course, I get it. I will make sure I make an appointment with my doctor this week. I'll take whatever you can give me for now." Fran turns and rustles through the cabinet behind her, then returns to me with a small box.

"Here, these are natural sleep hormone pills, but they still work well. You can take up to three." I slip the box from her grip and hand over my card, with anxiety starting to feed into my limbs. The afternoon was creeping on, and nighttime was drawing closer.

"Everything okay? You look like shit," Fran whooshed out in one breath.

"Yep, all good, Fran. Just need extra sleep so I am not dead on my feet at work." Taking my card back, I slip it into my back pocket. I make it back home, shower, and then find myself sitting on the couch in my small living room. I am busy spinning the small box of pills in my fingers while chewing the last piece of quiche that I had made for dinner. Fuck it, I tell myself, then rip the box open, and taking out three pills, I throw them in my mouth before drinking down the remainder of my orange juice.

My fingers grip around my throat. Gasps come in thick and heavy, but no air fills my lungs. My mouth is dry and burns with every breath I take.

"Come back to me," the monster calls from the darkness. Shaking my head from side to side, I find my voice.

"NO!" Crows fly all around me; they seem angry this time. Not scared. They are getting angry and impatient at my defiance. My head whips from side to side as the crows come in closer and closer, more of them joining the group that every second passes. My aching chest reminds me I can't breathe, yet I am still not dying.

The couch cushions under me create a nest for my sandy brown hair. I lie here, on my back, staring at my cream knit throw covering the back of my sofa. My fingers flutter over my face as I brush away the strands tangled in my eyelashes. I'm awake. I slept. I let out a long, deep breath through my slightly parted lips. Turning my head to the side, I glance at the box of sleeping pills on my small, box-style coffee table. I remember briefly having a nightmare, and then it just disappeared into nothing. My body must have finally transitioned into a deep sleep, causing the nightmares to suffocate and vanish. Sitting up slowly, I cringe at the smell wafting off me. I am still in my work clothes, my hair is still in a ponytail—well, the remains of it are—and I still smell of fries and roasted coffee.

I make my way to the bathroom after flicking the kettle on in the kitchen on the way past. I feel good and rested. My head isn't as loud as it normally is, and the fear usually following me around in the mornings isn't here haunting me. The shower is a comfort, relaxing me even more. I lather my foam cleanser over my face, happy to replace my work odor with fresh rose-scented facial products. Half an hour later, I am out the door, throwing my hair into a bun with my oversized scrunchy and walking beside my small cottage to where my single garage is situated. I don't drive often; there's no need to when everything is within walking distance. But today I am seeing Mom for her birthday, and she is farther out of town. I open my garage roller door, then unlock the driver's door to my small Kia hatchback. It starts with a protesting grunt, and then I pump the gas, letting the old engine roar to life. I roll out of the small garage space and onto the road. After pushing the button on my remote to close the garage door, I start towards the florist.

"Birdie love, your flowers are right here waiting for you," the florist says in greeting as I walk in. A smile stretches wide over my teeth when the bright arrangement catches my eyes. The gerberas are a mixture of pinks, yellow, and some white.

"They are perfect," I breathe and run my fingers delicately over the petals, watching them dip and bounce back up under my fingers' movements.

"Of course, they are perfect. They are for your beautiful momma," she says lovingly. I nod in agreement but feel choked up, and words escape me. I have been missing Mom more and more lately. She is the only person I can tell about my nightmares. I leave the florist and make my way out to where Mom is. I park my car and stare out my windscreen, grimacing at the sight. This is Mom's first birthday here, and I feel sick to my stomach. The ebbing of constant heartache and loneliness cracks through into a deep sorrow that hits me like a freight train. Tears run down my cheeks, so I quickly swipe them away. Birthdays are meant to be happy, and Mom will be pleased with her birthday flowers. That's all that matters now. I climb out of my car, flowers firmly in my hand, and walk up the gravel footpath. Stones make loud crunching noises under my runners with every step I make closer to Mom. I turn right, walk up a freshly mowed grass lane, and stop short. Sucking in a breath and then letting out a loud sob, Mom's shiny, beautiful headstone is in front of me. She has been out of my life for six months. Six months of being on my own without my best friend. In six months, I have had my 21st birthday, taken over our house on my own, cleared out her belongings, and gone full time at work to support myself. But this is the first time in six months I have been left completely speechless since her death.

I glance around the empty cemetery, eventually flicking back to Mom's headstone and the lily of the valley flowers at its base. She hates lilies of the valley. But only I know that. She said if she could rid the world of one single flower type, it would be them. So why are they sitting on her gravesite? Bile rises in my throat, and I have to force myself to swallow it back down, gagging at the taste and burning as it goes back down to my stomach. I sink to my knees, take the stems in my hand, then study the tiny white flowers. I always thought they were delicate and pretty. But Mom seemed to have a deep, running anger towards them. Placing them on the ground at my side, I replace them with the gerberas I have brought for her.

"Happy birthday, Mom. I miss you. And I promise these lilies will be going in the nearest bin," I say with a tremble of sorrow. Not in any rush to leave, I start picking at the blades of grass where I sit. I bask in the silence and bird song coming through the trees surrounding the small town cemetery.

"I wish you were here, Mom, I know you would let me sleep with you every night until these nightmares pass. Life is a real bitch sometimes," I mumble to myself while still picking at the grass, lost in thought.

"Ahem," comes a throat clear behind me. I jump, letting off a small squeak at the same time. "Sorry, I didn't mean to startle you," the deep voice offers. I frown angrily because I know that prying voice. I stand and turn to see Axel standing there, dressed in faded washed jeans and a black muscle top. His arms are pleasantly chiseled, and his skin is completely bare of any tattoos or markings.

"Are you following me?" I ask, letting my pissed-offness coat my words.

"No, sorry, Birdie. I am here seeing an old relative's gravesite. Just as you are?" He says, but the last bit is a question left hanging between us.

"My Mom. I'm visiting my Mom."

"Oh, sorry. Some sweet-lookin' flowers have fallen off her headstone. Here, let me put them back for you," he says as he moves to bend down.

"No, leave them. I am throwing them away."

"Oh, shame. These flowers have always been my favorite," he says while straightening back up. His presence is overwhelming, and I don't like people in my personal space.

"My Mom hates them, and so do I. If you love them, why don't you take them?" I say loudly over my shoulder as I start pacing away, back towards my car. The more space I can create between us, the better. I get one yard away before Axel is in step beside me, matching my fast pace and the lilies hanging in one of his hands.

"I hope I didn't overstep. I saw you here alone, so thought I would say hi."

"Do you not think if someone is alone at a cemetery, sitting in front of a gravestone, then they probably want to be there alone?" I say, feeling irritated. I was being unfair to Axel, but I still had no idea who put the lilies on Mom's resting place, and it sent chills up my spine.

"I get it. I truly am sorry." I stop in front of my car before I turn to Axel.

"I'm sorry, too. I am having a real shitty time at the moment. I'm not usually such a bitch." Axel's towering frame blocks the sun, casting a shadow over me while his eyes rake over me. "Nah, I don't think you're a bitch," he says, followed by a gentle smile.

"Wow, that B word really sounds harsher coming from a man," I chuckle quietly, more to myself. "So, where are you going after this?" he asks, changing the subject while crossing his arms over his impressive chest.

"I am thinking of taking this stranger Axel for lunch so I can pry into his life and distract myself from my own shambles." I suggest, feeling so brave for asking.

"This stranger Axel may agree if you are willing to jump on his Harley," he counters and nods his head to the other side of the car park. I glare across the space and see the same Harley as yesterday sitting in an empty corner of the car park. I swing my eyes back up to his beaming face and pout.

"No deal. You can fold your hefty limbs into my small car, or I will have lunch by myself," I shrug and push the unlock button on my car keys. Stepping around him, I head towards the driver's side and turn my back on Axel. I hear a deep sigh behind me and the knocking of heavy boots against concrete.

"You are very stubborn, Birdie. Maybe one day you will get on my bike," he says, sounding exasperated. I peer over the roof of the car, winking at Axel, already feeling myself warming up to the unfamiliar face. I've seen the same faces since I was four years old, so this is excitement I haven't had the pleasure of experiencing.

"I feel safer in the small metal box. I am a person that likes certain things in certain ways. Now, I will take you to a place that makes the nicest Caramel Cookie with just the right amount of sweetness." Something in that seemed to make Axel pleased. Because he nodded to me with a look of acceptance on his face as if I had said something he had been hoping to hear.

"Let's go then. I will be the judge of the Caramel Cookie."

The waves crash against the waterfront bakery. The smell of salt air is pungent. Axel and I sit at the small round, terracotta table in front of the busy bakery, each with a Caramel Cookie. I watch eagerly as Axel breaks a small piece off with his fork and scoops it into his mouth. I can feel my eyes, unblinking, zoning in on his every movement.

"You are making me feel self-conscious about chewing," he says between the big mouthful of slice.

"So... how is it?" I ask eagerly. Swallowing the large mouthful down, he leans back in his seat, crossing his arms once more.

"Well, I have had worse," he says. My mouth falls open, and then closing it, I lean back in my seat, mimicking his movements.

"You have horrible taste then." A chuckle comes from his big frame, and then he shakes his head.

"I'm kidding, it was beautiful. But I will also be honest with you. It's the first tan slice I have ever tried."

"Are you joking?"

"Nah, we don't eat much cake where I come from," he says seriously while looking out toward the ocean before continuing.

"In fact, this is the first time I have ever seen the ocean."

"Jesus, really? Do you live in the middle of nowhere?"

"Something like that. Just a tight-knit community like this, but more inland."

"Is it far from here?"

"Yeah, a few hours' ride. We like to keep to ourselves, but I wanted to stop here and see some family."

"Who's your family? I probably know them."

"Nah, they don't live here anymore. Just a long lost dead relative is all that is left."

"That's a shame. How long are you staying for?"

"Depends..."

"On?"

"When I can tie up some business. Now, can I ask about you?"

"Sure, since you love to pry anyway?" I answer, joking about our earlier exchanges.

"Do you have anyone special in your life?" That catches me off guard, but probably more because I have no experience meeting new people and opening up to new friends.

"Nah, it was just me and Mom for a long time. She passed away six months ago from liver cancer. Now it's just me and my friends in this town, of course. They look after me a lot." A shadow of disapproval crosses Axel's face before he clears his throat and smoothes his features.

"Have you ever thought of leaving Coastal Town?" He asks, taking another bite of the slice. I shake my head slightly and watch him with peaked interest.

"Nah, not really. I have no reason to leave. I have no other family."

"You would like where I live. Everyone is friendly, and they stick to strict routines. We live a simple life, but one that makes sense."

"What, like hippies or something?"

"Or something..." He chuckles before his phone starts ringing and interrupts us.

"I have to take this. Give me a minute," he says when he studies the phone screen. Axel slips off the chair and paces three big strides to the rail on the balcony that looks over the ocean. I watch his backside as his jeans tighten with him bent over the rail. His top is tight and molded around his muscles. I chew my bottom lip. He's a nice man, very handsome, but he doesn't set my body alight with desire. Maybe I have watched too many movies, but in them, there is always an explosive sexual tension between the man and woman. I'm no virgin, but I want more than drunken one-night stands. I am at the point in my life where I need a deeper connection and hot-steaming chemistry. He comes back a moment later, sitting back down.

"I have to cut our lunch short, sorry."

"That's okay, I will take you back to your bike." I make the move to stand up first and start walking down the wooden boardwalk that goes along the length of the few eateries. The car park comes into view, and as my eyes land on my car, I feel a twinge of regret over our ending hangout session. Because instantly my mind goes to the fact it's nearing the afternoon and after the afternoon is night time. The time of the day I dread.

"You are an intriguing woman, Birdie," Axel says as we walk toward my car.

"Well, you know where I work if you want to pop in to see me tomorrow. If you're still in town, that is." I look up to Axel's face when no answer follows, and a frown is fixed deep on his forehead.

"Is there something wrong?"

"Nope. I will try to see you tomorrow." He replies but seems unsure of his words. Maybe he has forgotten where I work. We make our way back to the graveyard with just the hum of soft music from the radio filling the silence. It was nice having a companion for the morning. I pull up alongside his shiny Harley, admiring it for a moment. If only I wasn't such a chicken, I would climb on the back of it. Feeling the wind through my long hair would be freeing, to say the least. "Are you having a quiet night in tonight?" Axel awkwardly asks me as his hand is wrapped around the door handle, ready to open it.

"Yeah, I have work tomorrow, so I will be home…" He nods his head as if impressed with my answer.

"I will catch you tomorrow, Birdie." I watch Axel climb onto his Harley, starting it instantly, and then my ears are filled with a deafening roar. He walks the bike backward, turning it slightly as he goes, and then without another look in my direction, he speeds off through the car park and out onto the main road, leaving me looking through my rearview mirror in utter awe, confirming that I would be in hell before I got on the back of that big beast. I make it back home five minutes later, backing my car into my single garage. It is just creeping on noon, but I'm not ready to be home yet. I make the quick decision that I will, for the first time in a very long time, go out to the local tavern. I'm sure I can convince one of the old coots to have a drink with me and play a round of pool. I loved playing pool with Mom growing up. I slam the car door behind me, jogging inside. I throw my keys on the hallway shelf and then stroll into my bedroom. I flick through some dresses hanging on my wardrobe rail, pushing each one to the side until my short black one catches my eye. I should wear happy, bright colors for Mom's birthday, but I am in the mood for something a little darker and more freeing. I strip off my cut-offs and white, floral singlet and slip my t-shirt-style black dress over my head. Shimmying into it and tugging the hem around my mid-thigh, I do a slow turn in my full-length mirror. I feel rebellious. I am twenty-one, for god's sake, and with nothing holding me back, but I have always been the cute small-town girl who wears sweet, beachy vibe clothes. I have been saving this dress for a special occasion, and it seems like tonight is the night. What's the point in hanging around home all night, dwelling on the monsters that haunt me in my sleep? After slipping my feet into my white runners, I make my way towards town.

Stale beer and greasy, deep-fried food hit my nostrils before I have fully opened the door. Jukebox music is blaring in the background, and the deep laughter of old men is coming from the tavern.

"Birdie! This isn't where you normally spend your days off." Old man Robert calls out from the booth occupied with all his friends.

"Felt like a beer," I shrug one shoulder gently, then flick my hair over my shoulder.

"Fair enough, girl. Save a dance for this old man before you head home."

"I might need a few more beers for that," I tease back before approaching the bar. Laughter erupts from the booth, causing me to roll my eyes at the dirty old men. Surprisingly, Axel catches my eye at the end of the bar. Not seeming the type to be at a bar drinking alone, I study him for a moment. He is nursing a beer in his large hands, lost in heavy thoughts, and is back to being the dark, moody Axel I first met. I also thought he had business to take care of. I stroll down the length of the bar, past all the high stools, while running my hand along the polished, stained countertop as I go. Axel doesn't bother to look up when I approach. His head is down, his hands spinning his beer around in circles. I sit beside him but feel his body tense, yet he doesn't stop spinning the tall class. It makes a soft, grinding noise with every turn, stealing all of Axel's focus.

"I thought you had business?" I start the conversation first.

"Felt like a drink." The short four words begrudgingly slip from his lips.

"Something wrong?"

"Nope."

"Well, aren't you Mr. Talkative now," I scornfully retort, regretting my decision to sit next to him. "Can I have a beer, please?" I call out to the bartender. She pours one and slides the glass across to me while I slide cash over at the same time.

"Maybe I will go sit with the old geezers. Least they will offer me conversation." I get up to leave, but Axel's hand shoots out, clamping around my arm to pull me back down.

"It wouldn't be a good look," he says, still refusing to make eye contact. I scoff loudly, then take a mouthful of beer. The soft, bubbly liquid feels like a pacifier to my mood. Once I have swallowed it down, I cross my feet at the ankles and start wiping away the condensation forming on my glass.

"You know, everyone in this town is like family. It wouldn't look out of place if I sit with them and drink a beer."

"Gotta love a close-knit community, huh," he grunts and leans his head back to take a long swig. His neck muscles ripple, his Adam's apple bobbing in his throat. My eyes become mesmerized with the movements, like a cat stalking its prey. I could almost swear Axel has gotten bigger, more ripped since I saw him only an hour or so ago.

"I thought you love a close-knit community. You were all for me meeting yours," I murmur, forcing my eyes back to my beer. A quiet snort comes from Axel as he shuffles in his seat slightly.

"I'm sure I was." Axel is back to being unreadable and mysterious. I am sick in the head because when he acts like this, my body seems to react like a drug addict seeking its next fix. And my next fix is in the form of the grumpy 6-foot brunet man beside me. I want to lean to the side to smell his leather jacket, but I stop myself.

"Do you play pool?" I ask him while looking over toward the unoccupied pool table. Axel lifts his head for the first time, tilting it to the side and toward the table. The hanging fluorescent lights highlight the specks of light brown in his eyes, and his thick brows furrow tightly.

"Can't say I have ever played. But doesn't look that hard?"

"You own a Harley and drink at bars alone, but you have never played pool? I will never understand you."

"It's best if you stop trying to understand me. One game..." he murmurs, then downs the last of his beer before slamming it down. The glass makes a loud clunking sound on the bar, with the ripped cords of muscle on his neck flexing with the movement. I down my near-full glass while trying to sedate my now dry, parched mouth. An unladylike belch erupts from my mouth, and I wipe my lips with the back of my hand.

"Don't judge me. It has been a weird week. Two more beers, please," I order and hold up two fingers to the bartender.

"Yeah, no kidding," Axel sighs, then walks over to the pool table, brushing his large hands through his hair. I grab the two tall beer glasses off the bar while watching Axel's movements.

He removes his jacket and places it on the bar leaner beside him. His shoulders stretch, muscles flexing under his tight shirt. There's something broken in me because when Axel acts dark and unfriendly like this, my body becomes heated, and my mind can't get past the image of his large arms tossing me onto the bar and burying himself deep in my body. My cheeks flush pink with embarrassment, even more so when Axel stands at the end of the pool table looking at me, head tilted with new peaked interest. I clear my throat and saunter over towards him.

"Do you know how to rack them up, or do you want me to do that?" Axel steps back and waves his arm out, gesturing for me to collect the balls and get the game ready to start. I pass him one of the beers, and as he takes it from my hand, our fingers brush slightly, and I clench my muscles. Axel pulls his hand back, taking a sip of his beer. He studies me over the glass before he diverts his brooding eyes away from mine. I walk around the table after placing my beer down on the side of it. Grabbing the balls, two at a time, I roll them to the half circle. The energy around us has changed. I don't know what changed it so quickly, but it is undeniable. I grab the triangle, place it on the table, and then fill it with all the balls. After removing the triangle, I walk to the other end of the table, placing the white ball on the small dot. I hand Axel a pool cue and run my eyes over his face set in stone. He's fighting what he is feeling; I can see the defiance on his face. But when he wraps his long fingers around the wooden cue, he meets my eyes with his jaw flexing. I can't help it; I smirk at him. My night just became very interesting. I wonder how long Axel can fight this for. I haven't flirted and teased anyone since last year. I have missed this feeling of acting purely on hormones and fuck the consequences. "You are not the good girl you proceed yourself to be clearly," he whispers in a rush beside my ear as he walks by me. He leans down and, stretching out, pulls his arm back, aims, and then smashes the white ball into the triangle. With a loud cracking sound, balls fly all around the table, scattering with no rhyme or rhythm. I nearly soak through my panties.

"All yours," he says, stepping back from the table and leaning against the back wall. I slowly look around the table, pick the ball I want to try and sink. I lean over the table, ready to take aim and hear the old men chuckling behind me. I roll my eyes and then focus on the ball again. As I pull my stick back to take the hit, Axel moves as quietly as a mouse and positions himself behind me. I thought he might be trying to flirt back, but I realize very quickly that he is angry at me.

"This game's over. You are not bending over the table so these old men can catch an eye full of your underwear," he seethes. I stand straight, shocked at his anger. I thought this was harmless flirting, but I guess I don't know Axel very well.

"I have grown up with them. They are harmless."

"If you want me to choke them all and gauge their eyes out, keep bending over the table." I turn to face him, but as I turn, I stare directly into his chest. I don't have the courage to peek up at his face. His chest is moving in and out rapidly, and I can feel his breath coming in thick and fast, blowing over the top of my head. I clench my hands at my sides to stop myself from running them over his chest. His pecs look as hard as steel, and every part of my body is screaming at me to find out for sure. Axel places a finger under my chin and pushes my head up so I gaze directly into his face.

"I think it's time you go home, Birdie," He breathes against my face. I close my eyes as the air tickles my face, causing goosebumps over my entire body. "My body is broken because I am more attracted to the grumpy version of you. This is the sexual tension the movies portray." Axel tenses against me, bringing his face closer so we were nose to nose.

"If I was you, I would never say that to me again." He says before dropping his finger and taking a large step back. I feel almost cold from the empty space between us now. The shit he says seems like a riddle sometimes, and only he knows the answer to it.

"I came out to have a good time. It's not even happy hour yet, so I think I will stay."

"You're going home, Birdie, even if I have to drag you." The way he says my name sends a sultry tingle through my core. I swallow hard and glance around for my beer. Axel watches me grab the beer and then skull the entire glass down, but he says nothing. As I slam it down on the edge of the pool table, I swing my head back to him.

"I will take that ride on your motorbike now. Or I will stay here and drink alone. But I am not going home."

"Now?" He asks me, looking confused.

"Are you brain damaged or something? I told you today I will never go on your bike, but I am feeling brave, and I think I would quite like to... Now..." I mumble the last bit, losing some of my mental strength. Looking at Axel, I start to feel I am playing with fire, and I will most certainly be the one that will get burnt. He drops his head, chuckling to himself. His shoulders shake with laughter, which is a bullseye for my attention. Bringing his head back up, his face holds a mischievous grin and a twinkle in his normally brooding eyes.

"Oh, this is too good. My soul is damned anyway, and I am going to hell. Let's go." He grabs his leather jacket and heads toward the front entrance, throwing cash on the bar to settle the bill for our beers. I follow behind quickly, nervous but incredibly excited.

The afternoon sun blinds me as I step outside. I raise my hands to shield my eyes and look over to where Axel is standing. I release a long breath and stroll over to him before I lose my nerve.

"Here, take this helmet," He says, handing over a matte black full-face helmet.

"What about you?"

"You need it more than me. Put it on." He demands that sends a shrill of excitement through me, making me comply. I slip the helmet over my head, and Axel grabs the straps underneath to tighten it.

"It will be a little loose on you because you have a smaller head. But it's better than nothing." He explains to me before dropping his hands and climbing onto the motorbike. I climb on behind him and wrap my arms firmly around his waist. He walks the bike backward out of the park and then starts it. We make our way along the waterfront, heading southwards out of town. The pebbly sand and rocks form beautiful formations. The waves crashing against the land create thick white water. We keep going for what must be thirty minutes until we come across a small pub off to the side of the road. It's painted charcoal black with white and blue signage hanging off the balcony. *Pirates Dock,* it reads. Axel slows down, pulling into the small gravel car park. It's quiet. There is one single cab pickup truck tucked alongside the pub; otherwise, I notice we are the only ones here. Axel stares at the building, then eyes flick around. As if assessing his surroundings and taking inventory. I climb off with an excited skip in my step.

"Hurry up, grumpy, I'm thirsty!" I say as I'm already heading inside. For a large, brute looking man that would scare off anyone with one glare, he is acting like a chicken shit.

"I hope I don't regret this," I hear him snarl as he climbs off the bike. I laugh loudly as I head up the timber panel decking and open the door. Axel's heavy boots are loud over the gravel as he follows me. An older man is behind the bar, dressed casually in worn jeans and a button-up black dress shirt with his logo on the chest. His peppered gray hair is combed neatly backward, and he greets us with a warm smile.

"What can I get ya's on this fine afternoon?" his husky voice asks us. Axel's questioning eyes slide to me, waiting. I raise an eyebrow but shrug.

"Give us a rum since this place is home to the pirates," I wink at the old man.

"Of course, ma'am," he chuckles back. He turns to grab two short glasses off the shelf and then fills them with top-shelf rum and cola. He pushes them to us, and Axel tosses him some cash. We both take a sip at the same time. My eyes nearly roll back in my head. I love a good rum. Axel chokes on the rum and coughs into his balled fist.

"You okay?"

"Yeah, I'm good. Just didn't expect it to be stronger than the beer," he wheezes with flushed cheeks.

"You have never had rum before?" I giggle and take another mouthful.

"Can't say I have. Now come on, we can safely play a game of pool now I know there is no one to perve at you," I glance over at the old, tattered pool table.

"Yeah, alright, I can't wait to see your face when you lose!"

Setting up the pool table once again tonight, I steal glances at Axel when I can. He is such a mystery.

"You really haven't tried any rum? What about vodka?"

He chalks up the end of his pool cue, catching on quick and mimicking my earlier actions.

"Birdie, I wasn't even allowed to go to school."

I feel my nose wrinkle as I scrunch up my face in confusion. But I shake my head as a sigh escapes my lips and I watch Axel break the balls.

An hour later, two rums later and three games of pool, I am intoxicated and a not-so humble winner. Axel isn't used to losing; I can tell by his sulking. I shouldn't be rubbing in my thrashing I served him, but I can't help rubbing salt in his masculine wound.

"Come on, time to go. You have shown me how skilled you are with balls," he smirks at me and pushes me out the pub door. I stop short and lean my back against the front porch railing. He cages me in, hands planted firmly on either side of my hips, gripping the railing. He leans down and sniffs the length of my hair.

"I am very skilled with balls," I say with a slight slur in my words.

"I bet you are. My balls want you to play with them very badly."

"Why don't you let me then?" I rub the front of his pants and wiggle my eyebrows. "Or do you have a girlfriend?" He pushes off the railing and stands straight while holding a hand out to me. I take it feeling frustrated that he won't give me what I want. As we walk back to the bike, he grumbles, "No girlfriend. Just a lot of wishing things could be fucking different." We make our way back into town. The fresh air doesn't help sober me up, and when we get back home, I am still swaying on my feet.

"You went a bit hard on the liquor, Birdie," he says to me as he scoops me into his arms, holding me firmly in his embrace. With every step he takes, my arms and legs bang against his side, so I lift my arms and loop them around his neck. His body shivers under mine, and he glides up the steps and through the front door as if I were a feather.

"If you tell me not to do something, I will definitely do it," I mumble with a drunk slur.

"You're a stubborn one, that's for sure."

"I like routine and have OCD in some areas of my life, I think. But when it comes to someone trying to make decisions for me, I draw the line." The words slur even more as Axel places me on my bed. The mattress sinks under our weight, and I can't help but grab a fist full of his t-shirt and pull it against my face. I take a deep sniff in through my nose and exhale slowly. I am a fucking animal. And I am okay with that. Axel tenses before standing back up, towering over me. His eyes rake my body up and down. I can feel my eyes flutter shut, and I welcome the deep alcohol-induced sleep, hopefully free of nightmares.

"I think he is utterly delusional because you do not have a submissive bone in your body..." Axel mumbles, sounding fierce.

"Who?" I ask, followed up by a yawn.

"Unfortunately, you will see soon enough..."

Fuck fuck fuck… I sit up in a rush, drop my head in my hands, and then lay back down. I sat up too fast. I lay still, taking a mental checklist of myself. My hands pat down my body, and I am relieved to find that my little black dress is still on me. My head hurts, still slightly spinning, and paired with last night being a total blur, none of this bodes well at all. The last thing I remember is being on the back of Axel's motorbike. Details from our night hover at the back of my mind like I should be remembering something important, but the harder I strain thinking about my night with Axel, the more my head throbs. I creep into the kitchen to fill a glass with water. I snag the painkillers from the first aid kit above the fridge, and as I swallow them down, I lean over the kitchen sink, internally praying they stay down. I am picturing the lecture in my head right now that Mom would give me if she were still alive. She said drunk girls make stupid decisions. And stupid decisions get you into a world of trouble. Once I have braved a shower and changed into my work clothes, I tie my hair up into a high ponytail and then apply a small amount of mascara, hoping it will make my eyes appear a little fresher rather than dull and hungover. I slip my feet into my work runners and head out the front door. As the tips of my toes touch the first step, I let out a fearful cry and jump back. Scattered down the steps are lilies of the valley flowers. My eyes well up with tears, and I glance around the road and into the neighboring properties. I lean against my front door, hand wrapping around the door handle to make a hasty escape inside if I need to. But nothing is out of place. My uneasy eyes drift back down to the steps, assessing the flowers thoroughly. Someone is really trying to mess with me and get in my head. Some people in the town know that Mom hates these flowers, but they are not the malicious type and would never do something like this. I drop to my knees, the pain of the impact on the concrete slashing at my bare skin. I hiss from the pain but scrape my hands over the steps, bunching the flowers into a large pile. I walk over to the outside garbage can and throw the flowers inside, slamming the lid back down once finished. I suck in a breath, stare straight ahead, and walk across the road towards town. I will find a way to figure out who is doing this to me, and I will make sure they pay with jail time. There must be a law against this sort of harassment.

By the time I arrive at work, I have worked myself into such a tizzy. My head is spinning from the hangover and the flowers. I can't think of anyone who would want to stalk or haunt me in such a way. As the bell rings in the door, signaling that I have entered the café, Sandy's eyes flick up from the counter followed by a small wave of her hand.

"How was your night darling?" She asks me loudly, announcing it to the whole world as if she knows something I don't.

"Fine. I had too much to drink but nothing too entertaining."

"Mmmmm," she replies as I get closer and push my handbag under the counter beside her. "What does mmmmm mean?"

"The old fellas reckon you had some fun last night with a tall, mysterious stranger on a bike. Good on you, I say!" She giggles as if she is a teenager rather than a woman in her seventies.

"Those old coots talk too much."

"Well, your tall, mysterious stranger is waiting for a coffee," she half snickers and her eyes flick to the side, indicating to me what she is talking about. I am not ready for this. How I didn't see or feel him when I walked in, I will never know. Last night, his energy was so intense, so captivating, and consuming. I slowly turn and give Axel an awkward wave as he meets my gaze. A soft smile touches his lips, and the spark I felt last night fizzles out. Yep, definitely broken because now he is being Mr. Smiley Guy again, my body slips back into a deep slumber.

"I will be right back," I slightly turn my head to Sandy as I speak and bite my lower lip. Sometimes, all the town folk feel like my adopted parents, and I am nervous talking to a man in front of Sandy even though I am a grown woman. My braveness from last night has certainly depleted.

"Of course, dear," she says back with a smug knowing look. I push the seats back into their tables as I weave through the room, trying to act casual, but my palms become sweaty the nearer I get. I push the chair on the other side of Axel's table, grip the back of the chair with my fingers, and lean my weight on it. For once, I am towering over

Axel, and I hope my voice can come off as confident as my body right now.

"I suppose you are a freak of nature who doesn't get hangovers?" Axel tilts his head at me, taking a moment before answering me. He laces his fingers together and places his large hands behind his head. He leans back on his seat, and my eyes drift over his arms. The muscles aren't as apparent as they were last night, but I guess today I'm not acting like a horny bitch in heat. "Mmmmm, so much for a quiet night at home, huh?" he says with a slight tone of disapproval. I feel my face morph into a deep frown in my own disapproval. I will never understand this man. He's like a guy with multiple personalities.

"Well, you didn't seem to mind when I climbed on the back of your bike," I throw at him bitterly, with one eyebrow arched, daring him to say something back to me. After what feels like an eternity of staring at each other in silence, he drops his arms, placing them on the table before leaning on his elbows. His light brown hair falls to the front, slightly covering his eyes.

"Yes, that was interesting," he mumbles, then continues, "I have to leave town. Go back home to my family. I have had a real nice time getting to know you, Birdie," he says to me, with my name a hushed whisper from his lips. He says it seductively, yet nothing in me burns with the same need that consumed me last night.

"You could give me your number? We can keep in touch, and maybe one day I will come to visit and finally leave this town," I suggest, with no intention of leaving Coastal Town.

"You know... I know this is very forward, but could you take some time off work and come with me? Like a holiday? I know your Mom's gone now, and you said you have no family around, so it could be nice, and you could get to know mine?" My stomach churns at what he is saying to me. He says it so intensely as if he is putting some power into his words that will bend my will and make me actually want to go.

"I can't, sorry. I have work commitments and a house to look after. But leave your number if you want," I offer in a friendly tone, but I know my face has gone solid like ice. I push off the chair I am still leaning on and return to the cashier counter.

"You okay darling?" Sandy asks as her eyes bounce between me and the table behind me.

"Yeah, fine," I mumble before the front doorbell rings. I know he is gone. I must have upset him, but I don't care. Today's exchange with him just felt all types of wrong.

"Alright, Birdie, well, table two needs cleaning,"

"Yes, I will get right on that. No more distractions for me," I say quietly, walking away to clear tables.

I start stacking plates and throw the napkins on them before glancing out the window. Axel is sitting across the road, leaning against his parked bike on the curb. He is talking on his cell phone and staring directly at me. His face is unreadable, but I now wonder if I have given time to someone who doesn't deserve it. I was stupid to befriend a stranger. Especially one that seems to be able to find me everywhere I go. Maybe after my shift I will visit our local sheriff to put an order in place. Goosebumps cover my arms, even though the summer heat is beaming through the clear glass onto my skin. I stand there frozen with the pile of plates in my arms and watch Axel put his saddle back on his Harley Davidson. He climbs on, roaring it to life, and takes off, flying down the quiet road. He doesn't give another look in my direction, but something deep within me tells me this isn't the last time I will see

Axel. The entire day is slow; my mind is lost in thought, and anxiety keeps my vocals and body in a slow tremble all day. The only thing that reminds me that I am awake and this isn't a nightmare is that my feet feel on fire in my sneakers. At the end of the day, I say goodbye to Sandy and head straight home. My eyes crawl up and down the side streets as I pass through them, and my ears listen out for the roaring of a motorbike, but nothing is amiss.

"It's fucking Thursday," I growl to myself. I was meant to wash my hair last night! The small routine in my life keeps everything in my life in cruise control. I need it to feel like I have everything in my life under control. Ever since I met Axel, I have swayed from routine, got drunk, and been on the back of a road bike. I hear people change when they meet a man they fancy, but I never thought that would be me. Especially one I fancy and then don't about three times a day. I fly through the door, slam it behind me, and head straight to the shower. I am dead set on washing my hair tonight, then I will get myself back into a nice, regular routine and forget about Axel, who sets my body on fire and then ice cold more times than I can count. Half an hour later, my hair is freshly washed and I'm sitting on my couch eating ramen noodles for dinner. I slurp the last of the juice down from my bowl, set it down on the table, and then pick up my sleeping pills. I swallow two down and head to my bedroom, where I tuck myself into my bed. I lay in the middle of my bed, smooth my blankets around me, and watch the ceiling. It doesn't take long. The tiredness from last night's antics mixed with a couple of weak sleeping pills is more than enough to pass out instantly. I just wish it could have put me straight into a deep sleep, so I skipped this part....

"Why are you refusing to come home?" the monster in the dark asks me. Sweat beads on my forehead as my hands and knees protest in pain against the pine needles. "Leave me alone." "You are remembering who you are." "I said, leave me alone." "You're remembering where you belong." I stand up and spin to try to lay eyes on the monster that is determined to haunt me every night. But it's black. Everything around me is pitch black. The temperature drops until I let out a breath, casting a cloud in front of me. I gasp in the air, and my throat and lungs burn from the icy air. I start running, but my feet become heavy, sinking into the ground with every step I take. "Stop running, Birdie. You can never escape us,"

I awake, tangled in my blankets with my singlet twisted on me. I am sweating furiously, my hair sticking to parts of my forehead. The room is dark; it's still the middle of the night, but I know I am not alone. I can feel eyes on me.

"Who's there?" I ask, but the room stays silent. I wriggle slowly to the side of my bed, dread creeping into my bones. *Is the monster from my dreams here to take me?* I slowly wave my hand around, searching for my side lamp. My fingers land on it, and I push the button. A dim light illuminates the room, and my eyes instantly fall on them. There was Axel. And another Axel. Topless. My eyes flick rapidly between the two as I shuffle back until my back is firm against my headboard. I want to get away from them, but as much as I hoped the wall behind me would let me pass through it, it never does. My eyes drift down, catching the sight of their large hands wrapped around each other's hard cocks, slowly wanking them, but their eyes are lost on my face.

"There's two of you?" I ask in a trembling voice.

"I'm Axel," one says.

"I'm Luca," the other says. My eyes swing from face to face, and it dawns on me. The minor differences I had been noticing over the last few days. I had been with two different men the entire time.

"This has to be some sort of sick joke. Get out of my house," I screech at them. But they keep going, slowly sliding their hands up and down each other's lengths.

"You like what you see, don't you?" Axel says

"What's better than one hard cock desperately seeking to pleasure you? ..Two...." Luca's deep voice runs over my body. A pair of lust-filled brown eyes rake over my body, while a pair of speckled chocolate, possessive eyes never stray from my own eyes. I can only imagine how much indecision is flickering through my eyes, like a mirror into the darkest, kinkiest part of my soul. I have never been so turned on in my life. This is wrong. This is sick. But the idea of both these brothers' cocks deep within me doesn't make me feel sick and twisted. It makes me feel wet beyond anything I have ever felt. I watch as their large, manly hands stroke each other's impressive cocks over and over. Fingers firmly wrapped around their wide shafts. I have always thought of cocks as ugly things but necessary in a woman's life. I suck my bottom lip as my hungry eyes ignite at the sight in front of me. These two cocks were far from ugly. They are perfect and every bit beautiful.

"Why are you here?" My voice comes out weak.

"Business. But pleasure first," Axel says. I stare at him. Knowing now which one is Axel. It doesn't take me long. Because although he is good-looking and an identical twin, he has straight brown eyes that scream nice guy. When my eyes flick beside him into the eyes that are multi-colored brown, I see hunger and defiance. Luca is the one that makes me forget all my morals. But I would be lying if I said having them both would be a fantasy most women wouldn't turn down.

"Why are you playing games with me, though?" I ask them both but look directly into Luca's dominating stare. His head tilts down slowly, so is looking at me angrily over his nose. He shakes his head slightly as if warning me.

"Do you want him?" Axel asks me I say nothing but pull the blankets up around my chin, covering my body as if it will help stop this fucked up situation from getting any more out of control.

"I asked you a question?" Axel says, strained, wanking Luca's cock faster. Luca returns the favor, wanking his brother's cock with firm, fast strokes.

"I will let you fuck him if you agree to come with us?" Axel says and then lets out a groan.

"I'm not leaving Coastal," I say, but my eyes are glued to their movements. Like an erotic porno that I can't get enough of. I see both their cock tips glisten with wetness, and I lick my lips, hungry to watch them climax. There is a power in knowing it is over me. Luca pushes his hips forward slightly, and his brother grips them harder. He likes it rougher. He likes it painful. My eyes shoot to his own, and I see the heat in them like an out-of-control bonfire. I peek down at Axel's cock, and Luca is stroking his slightly softer with his own hips carefully rocking against each stroke. He's the softer brother. The one that doesn't make me want to climb onto the back of a motorbike. I watch them both, eyes constantly going from side to side, not wanting to miss a single movement.

"Fuck," Luca growls and shoots cum on the foot of my bed. Axel breathes in deeply and moans quietly as cum shoots out not a second later. Both men have each other's cum on their hands, and they hold their hands out towards me.

"I don't want to come with you," I say firmly, but I feel out of breath. Axel frowns, but Luca speaks quietly, almost regretfully, "I know," I crawl towards them. Grabbing Axel's hand, I lick Luca's cum off in long strokes. Luca takes in a deep breath, tensing beside me. I move to the side once I am done. My eyes crawl upwards, gazing through my long eyelashes and stare directly into Luca's face. I wrap my hand around his wrist and pull his hand to my lips. Not taking my eyes off him, I lick the length of his palm like a cat licking the cream. His hand is hot and sets my body on fire. Luca hisses, and I see his cock twitch and start to harden again at my touch.

"Fuck this, enough games. Your idea didn't work. Now it's my idea..." I hear from beside me. "What ide...." I start to say, but as I turn my head, my world goes black from Axel stuffing a pillowcase over my head.

"Sorry, Birdie, we tried to be nice, but it's time to go home to see your daddy,"

I start frantically kicking and punching, but my hands are pulled roughly behind my back, and then they are tied firmly together. The bindings are hard and hurt my wrists, but I don't stop trying to tear them apart.

"Luca thought maybe if you wanted him enough, you would come without us forcing you. Poor brother got it so wrong. I think he just wanted a chance to touch you before he goes back to playing nice," Axel sneers. Then continues speaking, but no longer to me. "No more touching her, Luca. She's mine and has always been mine."

"Yeah, I know,"

"You know? But didn't stop you from letting her get on your fucking motorbike. You always have to break the rules, don't you,"

"You said she was spending the night at home, so I went out for a fucking beer. Not my fault she showed up."

"Since when do you go to a bar and have beer? It's against the rules."

"As you said, I'm the rule breaker, remember."

I started screaming again. As I kick my feet out, I connect with someone in front of me.

"Get her fucking legs," I hear Axel's whiney voice.

"Nah, not allowed to touch her again, remember? She's all yours," Luca says, and then I hear his heavy boots leave the room. My chest is heaving deep breaths in, and I start kicking again. "Fuck it," is the last thing I hear before I feel a sharp pinch in my arm, my eyelids become heavy, and then the world around me melts away.

I don't know how much time has passed, but I awake with a pained head and bindings on my wrists and ankles. I am lying on my side, still in my singlet and PJ shorts, but the pillowcase has been removed from my head. There's a large Harley beside me, tied down, and a strong smell of gasoline wafting through the small space. My nose wrinkles in protest, and the offensive smell makes my head spin even more. Licking my dry lips, I take a moment to observe more before realizing I am in the back of a transit van. I stretch my head up and see both brothers in the front of the truck. One is driving, the other is in the passenger seat on his phone. I can't tell them apart when it is this dark, and their backs are to me. The van wheels start crunching, signaling that we are going over gravel. The whole van starts rattling and bounces on every pothole we hit. I start counting in my head since it is the only gauge of time I have right now. I slowly count to 624 by the time we start slowing down. One of the brothers gets out, and I can hear hinges creaking; then, we slowly roll forward. A gate? We drive forward again, turning constantly while going uphill as well. I roll gently against the hard flooring as the van comes to a stop. The two front doors open and shut without missing a beat. My fearful eyes roam around the van frantically as I wait to see what I am in store for. I don't have to wait long because the back of the truck opens with the boot door rising high. Axel stands at the rear, his body looking like an evil silhouette against the dark of the night. Luca is off to the side, leaning against a tall tree, arms crossed over his chest as if he is merely curious and slightly bored.

"Now, this will go easier for you if you just behave and walk inside. All your questions will be answered soon enough." Staring at him, I am matching his nervous gaze. After a brief moment, I suck in a breath, letting my bottom lip tremble.

"If I behave, will you not hurt me?" Axel is impressed with my answer, smiling wide as he nods. "Of course. The last thing I want to do is hurt you."

"Okay then." I sigh, pretending to acquiesce while internally giving myself kudos for my amateur acting skills. Axel moves closer to me. Crawling through the van, he grips my ankles lightly and cuts the tape on them. He sits me up, and I wriggle myself to the end of the truck so my legs hang over the edge, and my toes touch the ground. I look around and notice there is nothing but pine trees in every direction. The smell is so strong that it nearly becomes offensive. I side-eye Luca, who has a deep frown embedded on his face, but he doesn't move his posture. Sometimes, I wonder if Luca can read my mind and if he knows what I am really up to. Axel stands in front of me, holding his hand out to me. I slip my fingers in his, and seeing Luca grow still beside me at our touch, I chuckle. Screw him, and screw me for pretty much dry-humping his leg the other night. Standing straight now, I cock my neck from side to side, trying to roll some of the tension from me.

"Come on, let's go," Axel says, coaxing me around the van. I waste no time and pull my foot back and then swing it up as hard as I can until I connect with his crotch. Axel doubles over while making sounds that are close to retching.

"Fucking grab her," Axel wheezes through the pain at Luca. I glare at Luca fiercely, daring him to try to touch me. Shaking his head with shoulders still shaking from his quiet laughter. Oh, I love how I seem to be a constant amusement to this man. *Not.*

"Nah, I'm not allowed to touch her you said. She's all yours bro," My eyes snap back to Axel, who is slowly getting off the ground. I take two steps backward, trying to create as much space between us as I can manage. Twigs snapping and crunching noises behind me distract me, and I turn my head and see two male figures in the dark creeping up behind me.

"Welcome home, Birdie," one says and then stabs me in the arm with another syringe. My legs become weak, and I feel my body start to lose control of itself. As I start to collapse, Luca steps forward toward me, looking furious, but one figure behind me catches me under the armpits before I hit the ground. My eyelids flutter shut.

The room is dark, although do I really call it a room? It is large. I view around myself, stretching my neck as far as my restraints allow. There are long, narrow rows of tables and chairs up each end. The ground beneath my bare feet is cold and hard. My head falls forward as I try to get a closer look and see that the entire floor is made of concrete. I am no longer in my PJs but rather in a long white linen gown with strange floral cutouts down the long sleeves that taper at my wrists. My hands are tied together but resting neatly on my lap, with my waist tied tightly to a chair. Candles are lit throughout the interior, burning brightly enough that I can see the walls are made of old timber. The smell of moss is evident in the air. It feels like I have gone back in time. Like I am in a completely different world.

"You are awake," comes a slow, soft male voice behind me. Quiet footsteps walk by me, and then the scraping of a chair follows, filling the large dwelling with an echo. My eyes land on a small-framed, older man with white-gray hair and eyes the same blue as mine. He sits before me, crossing his legs and assessing me silently as if I am part of a test.

"Do I know you?" I suddenly blurt out. His voice seems oddly familiar.

"Sort of, Birdie," he says. I feel my face pale as my name leaves his lips.

"You are the monster from my dreams!" I gasp and start thrashing in the chair, hoping somehow the restraints will loosen.

"You have been dreaming of me? Of your home?" He seems more interested now. His eyes squint at me more closely as he leans forward.

"This isn't my fucking home! Who are you?"

"I am your father, Birdie, and this most certainly is your home. Your mother took you away from us. But you belong here; even your subconscious is telling you this."

The life has been drained from me, and I let out a sob.

"You are sick. No wonder Mom took me away. Let me go! No father would treat their child this way."

"Well, that's the problem. You have forgotten where you belong. Where you are meant to be. This is your home, Birdie. This is a place only for the pure."

"Pure? You are fucked in the head. Are you in some sort of cult or something?"

"It's not a cult. It is a way of life. It is disappointing to see you speak so rashly and cuss the way you do."

"Bite me, mother fucker." He leans back on his seat, legs still crossed, giving me a look of pure disgust. This is the only pure thing I have seen from him yet.

"It may take some time, but you can be reminded of our ways. You are of our blood."

"I'm not staying here."

"Birdie, the sooner you accept this, the easier it will be."

"You can't keep me prisoner here," I say, filled with shock and new understanding.

"You were bred for Axel, and he refuses to be with anyone else but you, the chosen one."

"The chosen one?" I scoff loudly. I can't help it.

"The one that was chosen for him. Your mother and Axel's mother were bred around the same time, and you were both born into our world under the promise that you would be matched. You are destined to produce the next pure bloodline to continue our ways."

"And who is chosen for Luca? He was obviously bred at the same *fucking* time." I emphasize the cuss word now that I know it gets under his skin. A shadow crosses his face, and his demeanor becomes tense.

"Luca is not pure. He will not breed with anyone. Twins are not common among us. There is always a weaker one that doesn't have the strong genetics we prefer for carrying on our bloodlines. He was much smaller than Axel at birth, so Axel always showed to be the stronger and more suited of them both. Luca stays because the mother begged us to allow it. He knows he stays without a chance of breeding or going through our rituals. He is not part of us." He scolds with a voice full of authority and no room for negotiations. My heart breaks a little at that moment, thinking of Luca and his sad existence. But that passes as soon as I remind myself he could have easily not stolen me!

"Well, sad for him because he is the much stronger and bigger one now, huh? He has pretty eyes, too." I try to brush off what he says as nonsense.

"Pretty? He has the devil's eyes. His mother had to go through rigorous rituals to cleanse her blood from his bad omens and become pure once more. She was blessed because she has not had twins since."

"Rituals? What? Like splashing some godly water at her?"

"Godly?" he asks with surprise, and then I see a darker side to him as he continues. "Oh, we do the work of the great universe, trying to rid the world of weak bloodlines and keep to our simple ways. We serve a higher purpose. We do the work everyone else is afraid to do. Look at the world you have been living in. Full of foul-mouthed people who are lawless. But in terms of Jesus Christ? No," he says before getting up and flicking his fingers to a door off to the side. Signaling for someone. The door creaks wider open with two teenagers walking in. Their facial features are so much like me it's eerie. They have their heads bowed and hands tucked behind their backs as they walk in silently.

"These are your sisters, Robin and Wren. Although by a different mother. They are your sisters all the same," he waves his arm out, creating a shadowed, waterfall-like appearance from his long, whitewash muslin sleeve. They both have hair similar to mine but with a slight auburn tone and are long in length. My stomach starts to twist in knots.

"You may greet your sister," he says as he places his hands on their lower backs, with them now standing on either side of him. My skin begins to crawl like a bucket of tiny flesh-eating spiders has been poured over me.

"It's nice to finally meet you, sister," they both say in perfect unison with soft, sweet voices. In different circumstances, you could maybe think of them as enchanting. I study their faces, watching the shy yet eager little eyes looking at me expectantly. I am sitting here, tied to a chair, clearly a prisoner, and they act as if this is normal. A happy reunion of sorts. If I ever thought for a second that someone here might help me escape, now I don't. They were brainwashed. Or they were happy to be here and as sick as each other.

"The only family I have is now six feet in the fucking ground. Fuck off," I bite out.

They both gasp with quivering bottom lips. All it does is make me roll my eyes.

"Don't worry, girls, Birdie here has been away from home for too long, that is all. We will teach her our ways," *Daddy dearest* reassures them.

"Have fun trying," the words leave my lips before they tug into a smug smirk. He pushes the girls to the side, and they both walk, single-file, through the side door they came from. The stranger before me crouches low, coming level with my face so we are eye to eye. He returns my smug smirk, leaving a chill in its wake.

"Oh, my dear daughter. I will," he whispers. Straightening back up, he looks down at me, showing more darkness than before.

"Axel, you may enter," he calls out loudly, his hands clasped behind his back. Axel walks in purposefully, now dressed more like Dad, wearing a long, flowy, white muslin top and loose khaki pants. He is still muscular and has a poster-worthy face, but I can see him differently now. He may act like the nice guy, but he is all for the cause. He is selfish, disgusting, and evil to the core.

"Is she salvageable, Great One?" Axel asks while standing directly in front of me, studying me like I am an experiment. He swipes his tongue over his teeth with a slight rock on his heels. "She is of our blood. Of course, she is."

11

I am led out of the first building and into a lawned area. There are kids, adults, and teenagers everywhere. Keeping their heads down when I exit the building, they act as if I don't exist. They're almost zombie-like. The smell of pine trees fills my senses once more, the cooler, crisp air making the warm, salty scent from Coastal Town seem like a distant memory. We are in the middle of nowhere; I know that much. There are endless small buildings, cabins, and outhouses scattered over about two hectares of grassy area. It is a whole township off the grid. In every direction I look around the boundaries, it is tree after tree—thick forest and nothing else. Axel grips my elbow painfully, tugging it with force.

"Let's go, my Birdie. You are in the barn until you learn some manners," he murmurs in my ear. I flinch, pulling my head away from his breath. Not wanting any of him anywhere near me.

"Tsk tsk, that's not nice. If I want you close, you will be close to me. If I want you to open your womb to my seed, you will open your womb. If I want you to sit unmoving for 48 hours in silence, then that is exactly what you will do. You're back in my world now," he boasts, then pulls me harder. My eyes sting from unshed tears, but I let him lead me away.

We walk through the small village, through long grass, and over a gravel pathway around the back until we get to the barn. My feet are in pain, but I refuse to comment or show weakness. I like to think I am strong and can endure anything. But maybe I am wrong. Every time my eyes well up in despair, I consider that they may have already broken me. Axel drags me over the rough, dirt ground. I glance around as we make our way further in. The chains and hooks hanging from the timber support beams make me swallow bile. I have a feeling it's not just animals that get hung on those. The dirt from the ground coats my toes, with the powdery dust getting stuck between the cracks. Keeping my head down now, we head further into the barn, focusing on nothing but the light brown dust gathering on my feet. Axel pushes me into a room that has a small cot in the corner with a wool blanket and a white pale in the corner, my toilet, I am assuming.

"You wanna know what Birdie?" Axel asks me with a much softer voice. It reminds me more of the Axel I met in Coastal.

"What?" I reply as I still take time to take in the basic home I now have.

"I was ecstatic to find you. My whole life I have only wanted you. You were promised to me from the moment I was born. We live simple lives and don't want for much, but I made sure you would be my only bride. That's the way it should have always been. You should be pregnant with my children by now. It would be much nicer on all of us if you try and follow our ways. I truly think we could be happy together."

"Why the lilies? I am assuming you were the one that left them for me."

He shrugs, giving me a boyish grin. "I was hoping it would gently jog your memories of home." he says. And he really means it. Gently? He sees stalking me and leaving creepy shit for me to find as cute gentle reminders.

"You wanna know something Axel?" I ask the same question back to him.

"What?"

"You and your brother can eat a bowl of shit!" I growl at him. His grin disappears and in its place is the fierce evil expression I have seen on him before.

"Your training starts tomorrow," he tosses at me, then faces outside the room, snarling, "And you are security, nothing more," before walking off.

I stand in the middle of the small room, watching him walk away from me, wishing more than anything I could hang him on one of those hooks he is walking past.

"It's a waste of time," a deep voice breaks my erotic-like dream. I jump, giving a small yelp at the same time. My eyes flick to the side, landing on Luca leaning against part of the door frame. He steps further into the entrance, his broad figure taking up the entire space so he is all I can see.

"What's a waste of time," I say, my voice quiet. My fingers curl in my long gown, trying to cling to whatever they can manage.

"Thinking you can get out of this. Dreaming of his death won't help you." I hate that Luca knows exactly what thoughts are occupying my mind. He reads me well. I would never think of myself as being stupid, though. I know there's no point in fighting and trying to run right now. *Where the hell would I go?* I roll my eyes to myself at my choice of words. I am in hell. I probably haven't been gone long enough for someone to be looking for me either.

"And what would you suggest I do?" I ask while my eyes roam over the black leathers he is still in. *Interesting.* He hasn't changed into the white, flowy clothes like everyone else.

"Just follow the rules and obey. It will make things easier for you."

"I was never one to take the easy way out. I'd rather die than be with him." He steps into the room, making me feel claustrophobic. His head nearly hits the soft, ambient hanging light off the rafter.

"Well, I would rather you weren't dead," he whispers, searching my face with his haunted eyes. He is noticeably conflicted, and although I know I shouldn't, I feel for him.

I stare back, into those haunted eyes, remembering what my so-called father said.

"Why do they berate you for your multi-colored eyes? I think they are beautiful," I say, completely lost in our world, as I always seemed to be in his company. I reach my hand up, wanting to touch his face, but his hand snaps up faster than I can comprehend. His long fingers wrap around my small wrist, and he squeezes before raising my fingers to his lips, running my fingers across his soft skin.

"Do you really think I want to be one of their loyal breeding subjects? They say I am here as a favor to my mother, but I am still here because they need me as their muscle power. And I am perfectly okay with that. The only thing I'm not okay with is knowing my brother gets to feel your wet warmth around his shaft, and I don't," he draws his words out, breathing them into my face. I feel my anger rise, now knowing he likes being here and that he thinks Axel's cock being anywhere near me is okay. I thought he was a prisoner, too, a lost soul that I could connect with, but I was wrong.

"My pussy may be warm, but in no way will it ever be fucking wet for him," I snarl before spitting into his face. He closes his eyes, breathing deeply, his lips in a thin, tight line. He lets go of my hand and slowly wipes my saliva off his nose and cheek. I watch the movements, chin up, still blazing with an unwavering anger. He opens his eyes again, narrowing his gaze. The wild energy is rolling off him in waves, and instinctively, I step back.

"Don't even think about running, Birdie. Because I will chase you down, and I will fucking enjoy it." His eyes darken as the words leave his tight mouth, as if he has a vivid image of me running through the trees and him on my heels, with excitement filling his eyes. Or am I imagining it, with the depraved part of me growing with excitement? Some twisted part of me starts waking up as if coming out of a co-matose state. My eyes drop to his lips, where those luscious words had left his mouth. His eyes stalk my movements, causing him to let out a disapproving hiss while stepping back.

"That's the fucking problem. This place is embedded in your fuck-ing bones, in your soul, festering away. No matter how far your mom took you, you can't escape it. But you're looking at the wrong brother, Birdie," he backs out of the room as if too scared to take his eyes off me in case I jump him. He leans on a hand that is stretched high on the door frame.

"For someone that isn't very close with their family and families beliefs you were awfully close with Axel in my room!" I drop my eyes to the solid dirt ground and sit on the makeshift bed, with my insane fantasy bursting like an over-inflated balloon.

In my peripheral vision, I can see his heavy boot with the toe pointed down, kicking at the dirt beneath his feet. Small stones and soil flick across the ground as a soft hmph leaves his lips causing me to peek back up to his face.

"When you grow up in this place nothing is too sick. I knew you wanted me. You made that clear on our night out. Axel is like a fucking child that would do anything for his toy. I made a suggestion to him," he shrugs before continuing, "since we were going to take you anyway, I thought maybe you would be willing to come with us if we could give you the night of your dreams. Too bad though, now I have to be a good boy again, in this prison, and watch my brother touching you while I watch from the sidelines," he finishes his sentence as he pushes off the door frame and walks away from me.

The next day, a small female child brings me a tray with a bowl full of oats that resembles mushy vomit with a sprinkle of bird shit. Gone is my nice small-town girl personality. In its place is a foul-mouthed woman who demands answers as to why she is being dragged into a cult that she wants nothing to do with. The minor keeps her head hung low, her shoulders slumped, and she wears the same attire as me. Her blonde, wavy hair is braided at her back, and her facial features are rounded from the little I can see. Wasting no time, she quickly steps back out, shutting the door behind her with a loud creaking sound that follows as the old deadbolt gets forced back into place. I got no sleep last night; I tossed and turned with the small wool blanket covering my almost bare legs save for a small bit of gown. My white, sheet-like dress reaches my knees, and although my arms are covered along with my torso, I feel naked and grotty. All I can smell is rusty farm machinery, stale hay, and the strong, earthy scent of soil. My bladder screams at me, begging to be relieved. I nearly double over on the edge of the small cot while I stare at the bucket in the corner. I don't want to piss in the bucket. I don't want to give them that satisfaction. I don't know why, but it feels like they are winning if I eat their food and urinate in their bucket. Glancing over at the bowl of food, I get up and kick it at the door while smirking. My tummy grumbles, not staying in line with my stubborn thoughts, but I force myself to ignore it. But, unfortunately, I can not ignore the urge to pee. I sigh, grip my dress, and pull it up roughly before squatting over the tall bucket. I grimace, wondering what has been in this bucket before my bodily fluids. I relieve myself, pushing it out as fast as possible, eyeing the door at the same time, knowing that someone will be coming for me eventually. I was told my training starts today, and I shiver, dreading what on earth that could involve. I stand and pull my very plain and very large bloomers back up. I have never felt more inhuman in all my life. My fingers press down the material as I look down over myself with self-loathing and frustration.

After the rustling of the jammed deadbolt draws my attention once more, the door opens. Axel stands in the doorway, although not taking up as much space as Luca, though. Nah, he is slightly smaller—weaker. He is a fucking spoilt child that is nothing but a sheep, following every word, every order, and every belief that this freakish place holds. His loafer-clad feet step in the oats. He pauses, frowning deeply as his face turns down to view the mess, then raises his head back to me, meeting my eyes. We stare intensely at one another for a minute, neither ready to back down for our own reasons. He caves first when he is over our little game. He pushes his hair back roughly with a sigh, like it will help relieve some of the anger towards me he is fighting.

"Not hungry? How are you going to bear children if you starve yourself?" he asks softly, but it comes across scarier than when he raises his voice to me.

"Fuck you and fuck your food," I shoot back at him, holding my ground. I can't speak in the same quiet, terrifying tone. My anger is all firecrackers that spit unadulterated fury from my mouth.

"Tsk, tsk. The first thing we will do today is remove those profanities from your mouth so it is sweet once more. Then, when you come back, I will watch you eat the food off the ground." He steps into the small room, getting to me in one long stride, and grips me around the back of my arm. He breathes heavily as he pulls me out of the room in long strides, making me run behind him so I don't risk face-planting. My teeth grind together as my anger increases. I get pulled around the back of the barn, and I look wistfully toward all the citizens that are in the center of the small village once more, busy with their various chores like robots. None look up, all completely unbothered about a young female woman being dragged around the back of a barn. We make our way around the large barn, feet nearly getting tangled in the overgrown grass as we go. A strong, floral scent so sweet fills my senses that it almost tickles my nose. With my head still facing down, I don't see the flowers until I step on one. I want to scream, but nothing vocal comes out as the vocals get stuck in my throat from the shock. Looking up, I see a large field covered in Lily of the valley flowers. Thousands of them, with a small cabin in the middle. Some might call it beautiful, almost picturesque, but this is chilling. Everything that man has said must be true; my mom must have come from this place, and now I know why she hated these horrid flowers. Making our way up the cobbled path to the primitive, timber-clad building, we are met by lines of males dressed in white on either side of the pathway. Their hands are clasped in front of them, and they wear masks resembling black crows. Instantly, I can tell which one is my father; he stands at the entrance, and his crow's head is bigger than the rest. We walk up between the row of men, nothing but silence surrounding us, with a soft wind sweeping through the meadow. Axel halts before Father, nudging me forward so we are side by side. "Birdie, today you will be taught the values and principles of our large family. Our old ways are embedded deep within you, and today, we will bring them to your forefront," he says, then steps aside, gesturing for us to go in and allowing me to take my first look inside the building. I gulp loudly, and my stubborn attitude suddenly runs scared, leaving me with nothing but dread. There is a large stone platform in the middle of the room, hanging lanterns from the ceiling lighting the room, but otherwise, there is nothing else. I try to step backward, edging out the door, but my father's overbearing presence shadows me, firm against my back, blocking my way. I swallow thickly before brushing my hair from my face and back over my shoulder. Stepping forward, I make my way closer to the stone platform. The room smells of old metallic blood. The men all file into the room, creating a ring around the walls so I am completely surrounded. Luca steps through the door, dressed in black combat-style pants and a tight black t-shirt. His heavy shit-kicker boots thud against the timber flooring. After shutting the door behind him, he leans against it and crosses his arms over his chest.

"Why is he here?" Axel's deep, whiney voice echoes, bouncing off the walls.

"Because even if he is not one of us completely, he still needs a reminder sometimes of how things work around here," my father says, giving Luca a strange look. It was as if there was a hidden message between the two. With understanding, Axel nods.

"My chosen one, I am so glad I have you back now, where you belong." he strokes the side of my face, running a finger down my neck and across my collarbone. I make a mental note that I will scrub the fuck out of that part of my skin later on.

"Now, this room here is the heart of our family. This," he waves his arm over the concrete slab, "is where you will give birth to my children. This is also where punishments are taken when any rules are broken."

"Yes, by the time we have finished with you today, Birdie, I can guarantee you will not want to step out of line again. I don't enjoy doing this to you, my sweet daughter, but it is necessary." My eyes quickly bounce between their faces as they talk, starting to feel numb. I think today, being completely numb will be the only option for me to be able to survive this.

"Bend over the slab," Axel says. My eyes widen as I hesitate, but he sees it in my face.

"Bend over the slab, Birdie. And you will learn to obey my every single command." My heart races and the pounding against my ribs almost causes me to be sick. The sound is loud, and my eyes search the space around me, wondering if everyone else can hear my nervous heart. I turn, angling my body to look over the length of the cold, concrete platform, and gingerly bend over it. I feel vulnerable, exposed, and completely at their mercy.

"You wear white because it shows you are completely pure and obedient," Axel declares loudly, lifting my dress to display my large white bloomers. Expecting some sort of warning, I let out a high-pitched cry as a hard hit ricochets across my behind. I don't want to, but there is no way I can stay silent. Realizing that it wasn't his hand that hit me, I try to turn my head to see what it is, but he pushes severely at my back, pushing me forward, keeping my head looking dead ahead.

"Why do we wear white, Birdie?" he calls out loudly. I am still in shock, tears streaming down my cheeks like waterfalls. I sniff, deciding well and truly that maybe I don't want to survive today. Another big lash whips across my behind, and I scream louder this time. I turn my head to the side as much as I can, and Luca's eyes are on Axel, full of rage. Like a storm brewing away, ready to erupt.

"I asked you a question, and when I ask you a question, you will answer me!" Axel yells, whipping me again. I sob openly, eyes still focused on Luca. He meets my gaze, a look of regret and pity consuming me. I don't want his regret or his pity. I want him to save me. My eyes plead with him, but he shakes his head ever so slightly, so only I will notice it.

"Why do we wear white Birdie?" Axel yells again. Luca nods his head, telling me to answer. Well, fuck him. I squeeze my eyes shut, waiting for the hit. Even though I am anticipating it this time, it hurts me and shocks me just as much as the others before. I can feel wetness on my behind from fresh blood.

"She has had enough," Luca's deep, gravelly voice fills the room.

"You dare step in when I am dealing with my chosen one? You want to undermine me and make me look weak?" Axel screeches with more tantrum antics. I open my eyes, looking at Luca once more. His jaw flexes, and his brown eyes are enraged, but his arms are still crossed over his broad chest. He can overpower these men. Why doesn't he just take me and leave?

"Birdie, why do we wear white?" Axel asks again. Something in me dies. Maybe, I will have to be the one to save myself. One day.

"Because it is the color of purity and obedience," I say, sniffing loudly at the end as if it will suck all my tears back in and lock the pain and sadness deep within myself. Luca's eyes grow wide when I answer. From shock? A whip comes again out of nowhere. Luca jumps slightly at the sound, but my eyes don't waver. His eyes become murderous, revengeful. I return the revengeful stare, looking directly into his, promising retribution on every single person here, including him, for standing by and not helping me.

"Well done, Birdie," Axel praises me, and for the first time, a heavy hit across my behind does not follow.

"Will you obey my every demand to please me?"

"Yes," I say firmly, with Luca still receiving the same death stare from me.

"And you will stay pure for me until I give you my seed?" He asks. My eyes widen slightly at this question. Oh no. They don't know? Luca sees my panic and understands.

"Shes fucking done for the day," Luca says.

"Your obsession with her is enough. Get out," Axel seethes from behind me.

"Just answer the question, Birdie," my dad's voice comes beside me.

"No," the words leave my lips, and I wait for the backlash. The room fills with murmuring and shocked gasps. He whips me again, and warm liquid trickles faster down my thighs.

"I'm not a virgin if that is what you are asking," I say again. Maybe they will just kill me quickly. Another whip comes, and I scream so hard my lungs strain, and my throat burns.

"It's okay, Axel. We have a way of remedying the undesirable situation. We can fix her physically for you, and I have high hopes we can also fix her mentally. She will be perfect for you," My father says to him like he is soothing a toddler. Luca steps forward towards me, causing Axel to leave my backside so he can stand chest to chest with him.

"Hands off, brother,"

"You really want to try to take me on?" Luca says. My father stands between them and pushes them apart with a hand on each of their chests. He is weak and small, especially compared to the twins. But his mental power and authority over everyone is evident.

"Luca, you can take her back. You can listen to her cries of pain when she walks. That will be your punishment for overstepping. Axel, come with me, son. We will make a plan with the doctor," he says, walking out of the hut.

Axel is overly smug, and the rest of the males follow a single file behind them. Luca comes over to me, bends down, then pulls my large panties up my legs and fixes them back into place. I hiss loudly as the material touches my wounds.

"I'm so sorry, Birdie," he apologizes, turning me around slowly so I face him.

"I hate you. I hate all of you," I scorn him between sobs.

"Hating me is much better than me loving you, trust me," he says softly.

My body's confusion is throwing me into a deeper turmoil than just the physical pain and betrayal I already feel. I hobble through the field of flowers, hugging myself with my arms. Luca keeps trying to put his arm around me to help me. I have slapped his hand away multiple times and now he is just quiet, steadily walking beside me.

In my mind, I'm growing with the want to kill this man more than the others. I don't know why, but his betrayal haunts me more. But my body, my body wants to gingerly shuffle up close to him, as close as I can get, and for his arms to cradle me. My body yearns to be in his embrace so it can be comforted. I fight the urge, though. He walks with me through the barn, and I eye the cot. How am I meant to sit down? Tears prick at my already swollen eyes, and I cuss under my breath.

"I will get you cleaned up," My head snaps up, wild and wondering if I had heard him correctly. "You will not fucking touch me," I yell at him. He tilts his head, sighing loudly, but then leaves me. He shuts the door, locking it firmly behind him. I stand with my back against the wall, I contemplate laying on my stomach, but the dress and panties are sticking to my wounds, and I cringe at the thought of ripping them off dried blood later on.

A moment later, the door's hinges groan as it is forced open once more. The same young girl from this morning comes in, carrying a bowl of water and some white muslin cloth over her shoulder. She places the bowl beside the bed, head still hanging low, just like this morning.

"I will tend to your wounds, Birdie," her voice sounds so sweet and innocent, causing a different heartbreak. This could have easily been my life. My mom was brave and took me away, but had she not been, I could have been in this little girl's position. But no matter how badly I felt sorry for her, I won't have her touching me. I couldn't stand it.

"I'll clean myself up," I say to her. She raises her head slightly, displeasure looking at me through her eyelashes. Her eyes are a beautiful hazel, almost like an autumn leaf before it drops.

"Please let me do this," "Leave us!" The deep voice behind her makes her nearly jump out of her skin.

"But Luca, I was asked to tend to her." Her young voice trembles in fear.

"There will be no punishment for you, young one. I will make sure of it."

She bows her head slightly to him, "Thank you, Luca," she whispers, then runs off, leaving us alone in the room. He shuts the door behind him. I glance down at his large hands and scoff. He is holding a new gown for me.

"Take your grown off, Birdie." His voice is strong as he gives me his order.

"Like fuck," I reply. Defying Luca makes me feel alive. I cling to it. It's better than feeling broken. "We can do this the hard way or the easy way, but either way, I am cleaning up your wounds. Now change into this," His scolding voice orders me before he throws the gown at me. I snatch it mid-air in one hand, then eye it warily.

"I don't want you touching my arse,"

"Your foul mouth will get you in trouble here, Birdie," I sneer because I hate that I love the way he says Birdie. It should disgust me, but every time he says my name, I want to run and jump into his arms, demanding my own orders be followed.

"I'm certain you like my foul mouth," I counteract. Very slowly, his eyes drag over every part of my body before landing back on my lips. He scratches his chin, scraping the two-day stubble loudly, then runs his hands over the back of his neck and holds them there.

"You have no idea. Now change... quickly."

"Turn around," I bark at him, trying to sound defiant, but I know my will is wavering, and so does he.

"As you command," he mocks me and turns around. I slip out of my bloodied gown and tug down my bloomers, tears streaming down my cheeks. Every moment irritates the gashes, opening them back up and causing a world of pain. I pull the new gown on and tug the hem down to cover my behind.

"I am dressed; now you can leave. I will clean myself." He turns slowly, brooding eyes drilling holes into my own. He pulls some dressings and cream out of his large cargo pants pockets.

"I will be the only one tending to your wounds, Birdie. And I will tie you down if I have to," He looks like he wants me to fight back. Like he desperately wants to tie me up. Like he will enjoy tying me up. A small sigh leaves my lips, and his lips twitch from holding in a smirk.

I glare at him with narrowed eyes, but he knows he has won this battle. *It's okay, Luca, I will win the war.* I climb onto my bed, trying desperately not to scream from the stinging pain. After placing my head on my hands, I turn my head to the side. Luca moves closer to me, kneeling beside the bed. It's so quiet you can only hear our steady breathing.

"Will you get in trouble for this?" I ask, staring at my piss bucket for distraction as Luca slowly pulls my gown up. His rough hands lightly skim over the skin on my thighs as he lifts it higher. I close my eyes, hating my sick self for even liking his warm touch on me.

"You feel it too, don't you?" he huskily bites out. I don't reply instantly because his comment reminds me of his statement at the hut.

"If you care about me like you say you do, why did you let them do this to me?" I ask, ignoring his own question.

"It's complicated. You could never possibly understand."

"Try me," I say before hissing when a wet cloth comes down over my raw flesh. I wipe my cheeks and then lay my head on the back of my hands.

"I'm sorry," he says, but I am starting to wonder if he is sorry. I can't figure this man out. He acts like he cares about me, but then, in the same breath, he acts as if he wants to cause me pain and likes tormenting me.

"Just get on with it," I sob. I can hear the cloth being submerged and pulled back out. Fast drips fall into the bowl, followed by the soft pouring sound, so I know he is wringing out the cloth. I grind my teeth together with my whole body tensing, waiting for the pain. The sting when the damp cloth dabs softly against the welts makes me jump on the bed, and Lucas hand presses against my lower back. Holding me still as he cleans me.

"Jesus Christ." I spit through tightly clenched teeth. The cot creaks as Luca changes his body position and shifts his weight.

He leans down, whispering in my ear, "Word of advice? I wouldn't say that here either."

He straightens back up, wringing out his cloth in the bowl of water once more and then washing higher up on my thighs. I hate feeling like this. I'm enjoying it; it's comforting, it's warm and soft, and my body is responding drastically. I hate myself and feel disgusting for responding this way. He keeps rubbing gently, massaging the skin softly and slowly.

"The blood has... gone down further," he says, voice now deep and husky with yearning. I know exactly what he means. I can feel the blood drying.

"I can do it?" I say, but it is more of a question. I don't want to look at myself. I can feel the mess on my behind. That is enough to make my stomach curl over on itself.

"I want to," his husky voice whispers close to my thighs. I feel his breath on my wet thighs, and I suck in a breath. He's enjoying this. Mother fucker is actually enjoying this. I am allowed to be fucked up and enjoy this moment between us because I goddamn deserve it. But he is on the wrong side. He is one of the evil ones. *He. Is. Not. Allowed. To. Enjoy. It.* Truth is, I am selfish enough to say nothing on the matter. When he isn't around, I feel either rage or completely dead inside. When he's with me, I feel immense rage or desire.

"Okay," His hand moves down, deeper between my thighs.

"You need to spread your legs a little," His husky voice almost grates over my skin, sending a delicious ripple to my core. I want to squeeze my thighs together, rubbing them to try to press on my swollen clit. But I fight the urge and shuffle my legs further apart. I feel a cold breeze whisper over my skin, kissing the wet patches from the cleaned areas, making me break out in goosebumps. A shiver spreads over me, making my spine tremble.

"Are you cold?" He stops, holding the cloth above my body so water drips onto my thigh and trickles down.

"No." The single word leaves my lips. I think he begins to understand my internal struggle because the air around us changes. You could slice the tension with a knife. His hand slides down, wet cloth in hand, seeking the dried blood between my lips. He rubs gently, then lets out a quiet growl. As if he is a possessive, predatory animal.

"There's a lot of blood down here," He says quietly. I don't entirely believe him, but I am clutching to all the good feelings I can because I am clearly a sick fuck.

"Wipe it all out," I answer with no shame in sight. An almost hiss escapes him as he rinses the cloth in the bowl of water before resuming his work. I raise my hips slightly as his hand snakes down lower, creeping towards my clit. He rubs the damp cloth on it gently, then without me really realizing how the dynamics change, he holds the cloth under me, and I rub against it. My hips move in an undulate, over and over against the cloth. His breathing is loud, and I wonder if he wishes I was doing this to him. I close my eyes harder, pretending he is under me. His hard, chiseled body straining and gripping my hips. Telling me to ride him harder. I moan as my hips speed up, the vision still at the forefront of my mind. I can feel my wounds spread and reopen as I move my behind rapidly, but something deep within me, a darker side of me, welcomes it. It makes me rock harder against Luca's hand. I feel his finger swipe against my buttocks and then hear a sucking noise. He has tasted my blood. The shock wears off really fucking quickly as I rock rapidly against his hand. It's no longer on the soft cloth. He has angled his hand slightly, so I'm rubbing against his knuckles. The feeling of the bumpy nodules increases the feeling. The pressure builds, with tingles building within my core and the stinging on my rear. The contrasts just add to my pleasure. This dark, soulless place is starting to wear on me and taint my soul. I can feel it. I am becoming more messed up on a whole other level. I rock hard, edging closer to the climax I desperately seek. Shamelessly, I groan and orgasm a moment later. As the lightheadedness passes and my breathing slows once more, I cry. Cry loudly and ugly. My still neatly folded hands beneath my head become drenched in my warm, salty tears.

"Get out," I growl between cries when I finally notice that Luca's hand is still nestled between my legs. I hate Axel. I hate this place. I hate my sperm donor. I hate Luca and how my body and soul seem to recognize and pine for him. But most of all, I hate myself.

Last night, when Luca stood up and left without a word, without even a look in my direction actually, I put my large panties on and lay back on the cot. I couldn't curl up into a comforting ball because my behind was too sensitive, and it would cause it to bleed again. I lay still on my tummy and somehow found a way to drift off to sleep. I thought of the hut in the middle of the lilies at first which left me with anxiety and dread. But not too long after, my mind drifted away from that, and I thought of Coastal Town. Would anyone be missing me, I wondered. My eyes grew heavy, and sleep came to me as I pictured Mom's face and replayed a memory of us at the wharf, feet in the ocean, as she told me a story of a strong woman who faced her demons and fought for a better life. I was so young that she tucked my hair behind my ears and smiled softly. A girl born for a sole purpose and promised to an evil monster broke free and found a new destiny away from the soulless.

I woke early, head turned to the side still, and my first sight was the bucket in the corner. Mom risked everything for me. Her stories and fears as I grew up make so much more sense now. I carefully stretch my back up, feeling like I am in a yoga position with my hands beneath my chest and arms stretched straight so my back is stretched tall. I twist my neck from side to side, trying to ease some of the pain from being locked in one position all night. I shuffle off the cot as best I can, but there's no way of getting off without putting pressure on my rear. My breath hitches as I sit up straight, legs hanging over the edge. I stand quickly, not wanting to wait any longer and put myself through any more physical pain than needed. As I stand, the dressings on the ground catch my eye, and I think back to my misgivings about Luca. He left so quickly and obviously angry at me that he didn't cover my gashes. Not that I wanted him to stay and do that. The thought of him putting bandages on me after what I did makes my cheeks blush, and my stomach churn. I pick them up off the ground, lift my dress, drop my panties, then put the sticky wound dressings on my cuts. I cringe at my handiwork because I did it with haste, and I know some of the sticky parts are stuck to my opened cuts, but I decide to deal with that later. Because as I drop the hem of my dress back down, there is a knock on the door. The same girl from the previous day steps in through the heavy door with a tray of food. It's the same breakfast from yesterday. A bowl of over-cooked-looking oats and a small glass of water. I look it over, and tears prick in my eyes. What I wouldn't give for a freshly brewed cup of coffee and to see Sandy at work again. It feels like a lifetime ago, like a different life altogether. But in reality, it has only been a matter of days. But does time really mean anything here? Should I just stop trying to keep track? As each day passes, the anguish worsens. I raise my eyes to the small girl before me and really take her in. Her eyes are defeated, scared, and hopeless.

"How old are you?" I ask quietly. Her shoulders slump a little more, and my heart breaks for her. "I suppose you're not allowed to talk out of turn?"

"Yes, ma'am, I am just here to provide you food and help when I am told," she says quietly, her long blonde hair creating a curtain around her face. She uses it as a security blanket from my intrusion.

"Well, you can leave my food just down there," I point to a spot on the floor. She does as she is told and then backs out of the room and locks it after her. My attention flicks between the bucket and the tray of food. My body desperately craves the relief of using the bucket and starving for food. I haven't eaten in days, and it is showing. The shock kept my hunger at bay, but now, nothing can block out the fact that my stomach is sunken, and I feel faint. I gingerly approach the bucket, lift my dress, and pull my bloomers to the side. I try to pee standing as straight as possible so none of it trickles backward and into my cuts. When I am done, I cross the space to the food and pick up the bowl of oats. I wolf it down before downing my glass of water. The rattle of the old lock on the door alerts me of someone. I step away from the door and tray of food and back up against the cot so my legs are pressed against the frame. Luca is at the doorway, full of nerves. "What?" I ask without hesitation. He steps into the room, peeks over his shoulder, and then brings his captivating eyes back to me.

"They are sending me away for a bit to take care of some business. You must do as they say, Birdie, to keep yourself safe."

"Safe? Lashing at my arse for training is safe?" My words spit through my gritted teeth. His eyes darken as he looks at me through a narrow glare.

"Trust me, it could be a lot worse for you. You could be with me." He says as if I should be scared. He always thinks of himself as the bad twin. The evil one. How can he not see that he is the outcast in this group because he is the only one here with the slightest morals? He could tell me he's a serial killer, and I would still follow him into the depths of hell if it meant I didn't have to be with Axel. I meet his gaze and can only imagine the emotions and fight playing out behind them, like a window straight into my sick and twisted soul.

"Don't look at me like that!" he snarls, clearly feeling conflicted.

"Like what?" the innocence drips from my voice. I'm playing with fire again, the fire being Luca. He pulls me close to him, then snags a piece of my long hair, wrapping it around his index finger. As he pulls it painfully, bringing it to his nose, he sniffs, smelling my essence.

"Like I will be the one saving you. Because sorry, Birdie, I'm not leaving this place. Which means neither are you because I refuse to let you go."

Tears well up in my eyes from frustration.

"They are giving me to Axel. He's evil."

"He's not evil. He's the pure twin, remember." I scoff into his chest at the sarcasm because I still cannot move.

"You think you're evil? Some sort of grim reaper? But I know who I feel safer around. And it's not Axel." He makes a noise of defeat before letting the next words slip from his mouth.

"I *should* help you escape. Imagining you with Axel is filling me with something indescribable. But I would rather you be here with him, where I can watch over you from a distance, than let you go and never be able to see your face again." He runs his nose along the hair, still in his grip, and takes a deep breath.

"Or smell you again. You say I'm not evil. But I dream of you at my mercy, taking all of me while I unleash the morbid parts in me,"

"You say that, yet my body reacts the instant those words leave your lips. The thought of Axel taking my body leaves me feeling cold. I may as well be a corpse under him," Luca's grip on my hair becomes painful, and my scalp burns from the pressure of the hair being pulled from the follicles.

"Don't ever use the word corpse to describe yourself. I will rain hell on anyone and everyone if you, my sweet Birdie, ever become a corpse while I am still breathing. And you don't need to think about being under Axel yet. You have some time,"

"How can you be so sure?"

"They will wait till you have had a period. It has to be at a certain time of the month, and they want to make sure you bleed naturally,"

"That's so sick and clinical," I breathe with tears running down my cheeks from the pain in my head. Luca hasn't let up any of his grip yet.

"You're telling me. If I had it my way, I would be fucking you every single day. Even while you're on your period," he lets go of my hair abruptly, causing me to drop onto the cot and my behind to scream in pain. Luca is in the doorway once more, gripping the door with his knuckles turning white from his firm hold on it.

"And Birdie? You think I was upset because he struck you? Because you were in pain? Truth is, I was murderous because it wasn't me standing at your back, punishing you." He leaves me, and I am completely speechless. My mouth is dry, and I view my empty water glass. Would I have cared as much if it was Luca punishing me?

I hear the sound of shoes shuffling on the dirt floor, getting louder the closer they get to my room. I wait quietly, waiting for whoever is here to terrorize me next. Axel and my father walk towards the open door, side by side dressed the same and looking utterly serious.

"Good morning, daughter," my father greets me.

"What's your name?" I ask him with no friendliness. I hate referring to him as my father. I stand carefully, trying hard not to flinch or show any pain on my face to give them any satisfaction. "You can call me father,"

"Nah, that doesn't sit well with me. Because a father wouldn't do this to their child. What is your name?"

"How're your wounds, Birdie?" He says back with a sharp expression in his eyes, reminding me of how powerless I am in this place. I raise my chin slightly, trying to look strong, but my options are limited. Luca's words keep replaying in my head. He said he was going for a while. He couldn't protect me before, but at least I somehow felt more at ease with him here. Now, I am left feeling more isolated than I have since I was taken. Axel steps into the room, tilting his head and eyeing me warily.

"Today, Birdie, you can have your first day in the village. I would prefer it if we didn't have to lock you away, and you can start staying in my quarters with me like a chosen man and wife should," I begrudgingly observe Axel and Dad, who I can see over his shoulder.

"No part of me wants to share a house with you, Axel," His name slips off my tongue like bitter venom.

"Tell me, Birdie, if I was dressed in black leathers and my name was Luca would your answer be different?" He asks me. I smile at him, madness starting to sink in. Cabin fever? Dehydration? PTSD? I don't know, but I feel like I am in my body, yet I have no control over what I am saying or doing right now.

"If you were dressed in black leathers and changed your name I could still tell you both apart. Luca is more of a man than you will ever be," I cackle loudly. The strike across my face comes fast. I cup my throbbing cheek as Axel lowers his hand. My tongue snakes out and runs along my bottom lip as I lick the blood from my freshly split lip. Yet still, I smile at Axel. "See, point proven. Luca would never strike me out of anger. The only time he would ever hit me is when I ask for it for pleasure," I cackle once more, losing the last of my marbles.

"Uh, that's enough, Axel. We need to remind ourselves she was taken from us, and her mother let them live a life of sin. She has had a life of free will and a free tongue. She will learn her place. Have patience, son." My father placates as Axel's jaw ticks as he grinds his teeth together.

"Let's go. You can help the women with laundry."

I am led to the other side of the village. The first day I walked through it, I didn't think it was big. But now, as we follow a path that weaves through huts, I see it goes much further back than I anticipated. We are getting closer to the pine trees at the forest edging. Birds are all around us, fluttering and singing in the trees like they are happy to share their home with us. I always looked at birds as sweet, carefree animals. Seeing them here, sharing space with people I consider the most evil that walk the earth, and happily doing so, I all of a sudden hate my name. Axel and Father are in front of me, shoulder to shoulder, taking me toward a long, narrow building that is now coming into view. Everything here is made of timber. The smell of wood, moss, and dirt surrounds me everywhere inside the village. But straight ahead, behind the narrow building, the fresh, crisp scent of pine needles fills my nose as the wind picks up and carries it to me. My feet falter on a rock, causing me to stumble and trip, falling into the back of Axel. He spins quickly, as if time has slowed for him, latches on to my arm, and fixes me back up. He glances down at my feet and scowls, unhappy with his observation.

"You need to wash, and I'll tell the woman to get you some shoes that fit."

"I'm fine." I sneer, not wanting to take anything from him.

"Your feet are bleeding. I won't have any woman of mine walking around barefoot and bleeding." I cross my arms at my chest and arch an eyebrow at him. Did he really just say what I think he did? He cottons on real quick and sees the irony in his words. But I am starting to cotton on to things myself and have a feeling men are never in the wrong here. *Even if they are.*

"Enough talking. We are in the laundry area, and everyone is waiting for you." He ends our exchange and begins walking once more. He steps into the building, and as I step over the threshold, I scan my feet and cringe at the sight. They are fucking filthy, and I am sporting a bleeding toe from where I stubbed it on the rock. There are five women lined up inside the building. Two I recognize from the other day. My sisters. Their heads hang low, perfectly in a row, and all silent. I look around, surveying my surroundings. There are large tubs throughout the area, filled with water, long wooden tables, and wire lined along the ceiling beams.

"Have we gone back into the fucking dark ages," I say without a second thought. Old habits die hard, I guess. If growing up, being able to speak freely is called living in sin, then throw me straight into hell because I am a straight sinner. The girls gasp causing me to have to bite back a snort. I all but roll my eyes and then meet the two pairs of disapproving eyes. I shrug at them. What else is there to do?

"I was hoping we wouldn't have to take you back to the ceremonial room, but tomorrow morning, you will be taking your punishment," my father says. Axel's face lets me know he is disappointed in me. Like he doesn't want to whip me. He wants me to obey and respond when he needs me. He wants a trophy wife in this crazy arse world they live in. The cuts on my behind remind me harshly of my whipping from the day before and the screams that tore from my throat. I can't go through that again. It'll be worse, too. They will be whipping across already fresh, raw gashes. *I can't do it again.* I'm on my own now that Luca isn't here. His words repeat once more through my mind like a lullaby.

"I am sorry for speaking out of turn. I will make more of an effort to fall in line." I say, sounding sincere. I am sincere. Sincere in the fact I don't want another beating. But the whole time the words are slipping from my lips, I can't help but give them the imaginary middle finger and hope they all drop dead in front of me from random heart attacks. My father regards me for what feels like a millennium.

"Right, let's begin, shall we, Birdie?"

I nod at him. Too scared to speak and piss him off.

"This is the laundry room. We have a roster system, and all the women take turns doing all the chores around the camps." Oh, the urge to ask what the fucking men do is right on the tip of my tongue. Like a spicy hot pepper burning it, wanting me to spit it out to relieve the pressure. Axel lurks closely, studying my reactions. Waiting for me to fuck up, or possibly trying to see if, indeed, I have surrendered and succumbed to their sick and hostile ways.

"You do not speak to one another. You have no business to talk about. Get in and get the job done. The women can then return to their homes and care for them. The only women not part of doing laundry are those with other chores, have just given birth, or are ill."

I nod again, staying silent. What a sad existence. No one ever talks? Surely, some of them speak secretly when the men are not around.

"The women have permission to speak today to show you how to complete the chores. But you will be a fast learner because today is their only day."

I nod, and they both walk out, leaving me with five women who are staring at the fucking ground still. I have so many unanswered questions that I seek answers, too. As they all raise their heads, their eyes meet mine. I glance from face to face. With mixtures of blue eyes, brown eyes, and green eyes, they all have the same theme, all equally timid. One of my sisters, Robin, steps forward and opens her mouth to speak, leading with a big breath first as if it is a foreign feeling.

"We put all the linen and towels in the tubs first. I can do the first lot with you if you would like?" "Sure, sounds brilliant," I say sarcastically. Her eyes widen slightly at my reply but she takes me to the tub down the furthest end. I help her throw an armful of sheets and lower them into the water. She hands me a large wooden stick with an encouraging smile.

"Put the paddle in the water and use it to push the towels around the tub. We do this over and over and slightly bash the washing with it, I guess, to ensure they are thoroughly cleaned." "Then what do we do with them?" I ask as I put the paddle in the water and start turning the washing through the sud water. It's harder than it looks, and my arms are burning.

"We then squeeze them out, put them in that tub there for a rinse in clean water, and then squeeze again before hanging them up on the wires. We also have lines out the back for when it's a really nice day, but we don't get a lot of sun because of the trees," she says quietly and curiously, still testing her words on her lips. I can see the unusual expression in her eyes as she speaks. I scoff and chuckle at us both.

"Well, I could have guessed that sun here would be pretty fucking limited."

Her soft gasps hitch in her throat, and she throws her hand over her mouth.

"Sorry," I say quietly. She stares into the water, supervising me as I keep pushing the washing around and prodding it with the paddle.

"So if you're not allowed to speak freely, how do children learn to speak?" I ask without meeting her eyes. Her face tells me how frightened she is, as if she is about to jump out of her skin and run away from me.

"You can answer me. Remember you are teaching me and were told you can speak freely?"

"I suppose Father did say that. The children have a school they attend. This is where they are taught the rules of life and how to live correctly. They are taught to speak, but boys and girls get kept apart in different classrooms because they have different rules."

"Huh, well, that makes sense. I guess. Do any more outcasts like Luca live here?" She eyes me and shakes her head. "No. He is allowed to stay as a favor to his mother."

"So if he wanted to leave, he could?" She becomes short with me and takes the paddle from my hands.

"It's done. We can take the washing out and rinse it."

"Sorry, did I say something wrong?"

"I don't like these conversations sister. But no, there is no leaving. Our family lives purely, and if those no longer want to live in our ways, then they are surrendered to the crows,"

"What? Like your god?" Her voice grows quieter. "No, I mean the actual crows," her eyes flick around when the words leave her mouth. I can feel the shock written all over my face. I knew this place was something I could never have imagined, but deep within my bones, I know that there is evil here I have yet to see. Part of me had been praying to Mom or any higher power out there to get me out of this situation somehow, but being honest with myself. I don't think Mom, god, or anyone good has any sort of power here.

Two hours later, my hands throb and blisters have formed at the base of my fingers. I am leaning against a wooden table, staring at my fingers as I wiggle them, grimacing at the liquid-filled sores.

"Your hands toughen up over time," Robin says quietly beside me.

"At what age do you get chosen for a male?" I ask before tucking my hands behind my back.

"It used to be at birth, but traditions are changing slightly."

"Why?" I ask, not understanding all the riddles this place holds.

"Generations ago, this place was founded by those who could see that the world around us is full of sin, and with the freedom everyone gained over time, our great-great grandparents could see the human race would become evil and destroy each other. They came here, settled, and created their own traditions. Apparently, your father's great-great-grandfather could speak to high powers who told him what he needed to do so all our souls could be spared and go to the pure places after death."

"Heaven?"

"Nah, not in the Jesus Christ sense. They don't worship that god. But anyhow, when they first started out, twenty different families came here and followed the orders. But over time, with the breeding, it's become difficult because you can't always guarantee one chosen wife will have a boy and the other chosen wife will have a girl. Also, eventually, bloodlines would start blurring. That's why they have so desperately brought you back. You were picked for Axel at birth as one of the last remaining who can create a new line. Your mother only had you before she ran away."

"What about my father, though? He is a father to you as well. Are there blurred bloodlines there?"

"Not yet. My mother was very young when she was chosen for Father. She had me and my sister. Eventually, maybe in the next generation, there will be no option but to start blurring bloodlines. My father keeps telling everyone it's okay because we are of the pure, and it's a way to make sure we stay that way, but I know it makes some people nervous."

"Ahem, it's lunchtime," An older woman says to the side of us with the short order. We both jump, and she gives Robin the most scolding look. One of the women pushes the laundry door open, and it slams against the side of the hut. I follow behind them, out onto the pathway that goes back into the center of the village. I chew the inside of my cheek, fighting back tears. I can feel my wounds sticking to the dressings. Tonight is going to be painful when I have to force myself to rip them off. I follow my sister, the only one willing to talk to me, through the village and to the largest building. It is the one I was brought to when I first got taken. The commotion as I step inside is confronting. Tiny toddlers are sitting quietly at the long tables, men are scattered around talking amongst themselves, and babies are crying, nursing on their mother's breasts. All other women carry trays of food, placing them in the center of the tables along with jugs of water. I feel the evil at my back. My skin tries to crawl away from him when he is near. I will always be able to feel him.

"Sit down, down the far end. It's time you meet my mother, chosen one," Axel says quietly in my ear.

"I don't want to sit today," I reply because the long timber bench seats are hard, and I know they will tear apart my gashes. Axel's hand is placed on my lower back, and I lurch forward.

"That wasn't nice, Birdie. Now sit, or I will take you back to the concrete slab." I listen to him, walking down the long narrow room, ignoring everyone, not that they look in my direction anyway. I gingerly sit on the seat, trying hard to not cry. I settle in one position, like a statue, because if I shift at all, I may bleed on the seat. One of the younger girls places a plate of food before me. Then, an older lady with the same square face and eyes as Axel sits opposite me. "It's nice to meet you, Birdie. I am Gwen," she says politely. It is like dating a man in college and meeting his parents at dinner for the first time. She takes a mouthful of her broth, then proceeds to tear some bread and dip it in.

"Why don't you have a bird's name? Seems to be a theme," I say and play with the broth. My tummy grumbles as the hot, steamy fragrance hits my nose, causing my willpower to vanish. I take a mouthful and nearly let out a groan. My cheeks blush as the thought enters my mind because I remind myself of Luca. I take another mouthful quickly, letting my hair fall around my face as I do to shade the pink colors.

"No, only the children of the leading fathers get blessed with bird names. I am very proud to have a leading father's daughter in my family. It is a blessing," she says. A smile spreads across her face, reaching her eyes. She's serious with her words. She means every goddamn word. Like I chose to come here? It's no secret I am here against my will.

"Well, where else would I be?" I ask her, replying with sarcasm, which is becoming my most common response when I feel threatened and pissed off. Gwen clears her throat and takes another mouthful of her food, ignoring my sarcastic question. I guess you could have called it a rhetorical question because it really didn't need an answer spoken out loud. We continue to eat in silence. I allow my eyes to drift around the room a few times, but it depresses me more. The men here talk and socialize like kings, even the male children. The women are empty. Like no one is truly home inside their bloody heads. I don't think they talk to gods at all. I think a long time ago, a man went on an ego trip and wanted to control a village of unknowing people.

Father comes over, grabbing Axel. They stand off to the side, deep in quiet conversation. I stare at them while I chew on a mouthful of bread. The bread moves around my mouth, and I force it down, nearly choking on the dry lump. I drink some water, but my eyes still never waver from Axel. "Birdie, you really shouldn't stare. You will get in trouble again!" Gwen hisses at me, not too pleased with my openness.

"It's clearly about me. How can I not be curious?"

"You need to make my son happy. Be an obliging and willing chosen for him. You need to focus on bearing his children of the pure," she scolds me like I have just cheated on him or something. I don't know if I want to barf or punch someone. Can they not see I am trying? The last thing I want is to be beaten again. I drop my head, scoop another spoonful of broth and veggies, and swallow it down. A red-haired lady across the table catches my eye. She is sitting with Robin and Wren. They have the same shape faces, although the girls have my father's features. Her eyes are stone cold. A hard, steely blue. She must be their mother. She seems so young. Much younger than Mom. I guess they would have had to pair him with someone fresh after Mom left with me. I almost feel sick. Axel returns to us and sits down beside me. My body tenses at his nearness. He is identical to Luca, yet the feeling between us is ice cold. Well, from my side, anyhow.

"You need to go to the doctor after you have been excused from the lunch table,"

"What for?"

His jaw flexes, and his eyes slip to me in a look of disgust.

"Can you not just accept what I say for once? You need to get your behind cleaned up and redressed. Your sister will take you." He is still utterly pissed off.

"Something else wrong?" He turns in his seat, looking me over.

"It will be remedied soon enough. The sooner, the better." He spits out before standing and pacing outside.

"The vibe here is all off since you have come back. The sooner they fix you, the better," Gwen says, standing not long after Axel's departure.

"Aren't you meant to be silent unless spoken to?" I raise my head so our eyes meet and lean my hands on the table so I am a fraction closer to her.

"We have a day pass for you. You are a firecracker like your mother. That didn't turn out very well either." Gwen says and walks away from me. It seems like a warning. Robin greets me at my back. I stand and carefully pluck the material away from the dressing tape where small bits have stuck. She sees my pained face and shows the real first lot of empathy I have experienced yet.

"The doctor will help with that."

"Thanks," is all I manage.

We head through the village once more. I think I am starting to get the hang of it now. We walk slowly, thanks to my physical pain, giving me a chance to look around. The largest building is the one we just came from. That must be where all the meals and large gatherings are held. As you exit the large building, the large clearing is the main hangout area, as I would call it which is also the first thing you see. There's a large fire pit in the middle, but it doesn't appear to be used this time of the year. To the left are rows of small houses. I can only imagine what the inside décor is like. Behind the houses is the laundry where I was this morning. We are heading to the right-hand side with extensive gardens, vegetable patches, and more buildings. If I had carried on straight through the clearing, I would eventually have arrived at the barn where I stay. Beyond that is a large field of disgusting flowers that frame a disgusting room where torture happens. The grass is overgrown in most places, and paths are dirt or stones. I have noticed pine needles are at the front of some people's houses, which they must use to keep grass down. We go past the gardens where women are gathering with baskets. Robin stops in front of a small cottage-like building in natural stained timber with concrete steps covered in a soft scattering of moss. It's well-built, and I can only assume it was one of the first buildings constructed here. Robin taps on the door, waiting for the door to open. An old man with near-white hair opens the door, his severely wrinkled face assessing me with no emotions. I am a subject, nothing more. Instead of feeling like I will get some much-needed help, I step back, not wanting to be anywhere near this man.

"You want help up the stairs?" His frail voice asks me. I know what sort of help he means. More horrid men manhandling me and forcing me to do stuff. I swallow thickly, feeling parched all of a suddenly.

"I can manage the steps just fine," I grumble, desperately trying not to let him know how much he scares me. The door closes, and I am left alone in the doctor's house with a man with the most empty eyes I have ever seen.

The first thing I can't help but notice is the surgical smell of bleach.

"Not so self-sufficient if you have bleach and surgical supplies," I mumble under my breath. We are standing in a small lounge-like room with a couch, cupboards, a small kitchenette to the back, and two doors on either side going off it. The old man, who had his back turned to me while rummaging in one of the cupboards, turns slowly, glaring at me as soon as his eyes seek me out.

"I have heard you are a talker," he scolds me. I shrug my shoulders.

"I can't help how I was brought up," I say, coming to my own defense, hoping he may understand. But this man doesn't understand any empathic emotions.

"You wanna know what we did to the last young mouthy brat like you?" he asks me, staring me down so much I feel like I want to shrink down to the ground to get away from his eyes.

"What?" I ask, although I really don't want to know the answer.

"I sewed her mouth shut until she forgot how to talk. She had to drink broth through a straw for a very long time. And if that didn't work, I would have removed her voice box. If you enjoy eating solid food, I suggest you forget about your old life of sin your mother raised you in."

My vision begins to blur with tears that gather, and I start blinking quickly, trying to force them away. The doctor turns back, wheezing and coughing as he does. Maybe he will die of old age before he gets a chance to stitch my mouth shut.

"Ah, there it is," He murmurs, turns, and holds his hand out to me.

"Get in that room, lie down and I will put this cream on." He definitely likes to speak words that are direct and straight to the point.

My shoulders slump with how defeated I feel. I make my way to the door that he is gesturing to and trudge into the room. A hospital gurney, lamps, and tables are arranged with medical equipment. I climb onto the small bed and wait. I don't want an old crusty man messing with my behind. But whatever dignity I once had, it is now long gone. Maybe this is how the women here have become how they are. Their dignity gets completely stripped from them right from the start, so the only way of living that they know is one of submission and shutting the fuck up. I hear the old man's shuffling footsteps come into the room, and he immediately goes to work. He lifts my dress up and pulls my panties down. He's not kind about it either.

"Ow!" I cry out when the undies that are stuck to some of the blood-soaked pads pull at them. "Pain is all in your head. Next time you make a noise, I will request your lips be shut!" his growl fills the room before he rips the dressings off. I bite my tongue. My tight, stressed chest rises and stays there as I hold my breath. I am frozen in place, chest full of air, tongue now bleeding under the pressure of my teeth. Another ripping noise fills the room as the dressing pad I had placed incorrectly, with the tape stuck to raw skin, comes off at a shattering pace. Tears slip down my cheeks, almost tickling them. I now slowly let out the breath I have held, and I swallow down my own blood. My tongue already feels swollen and I don't think anyone needs to worry about me speaking now because I don't think I physically can. Ointment gets smeared over my gashes. I tense my arse cheeks as the salve causes a sharp stinging. My hands scratch at the bed beside my head. I try to fight it, but human reaction takes hold of my body; it is just another thing in my life that parts me of my free will. I feel the cool touch of wound dressings being placed over my now clean gashes. As I lay feeling the doctor's work, I wonder if joining my mom in death would be a privilege right now. Would being reunited with her and taken from this hell be a gift? We were always taught growing up that hell was fire, burning, and pained screams. Now I know it was all a lie. Hell is cold, isolating, and deep within a pine forest full of sinister men who take what they want when they want.

"You are done," the doctor says, and I hear him take off his disposable gloves, which sound sickly rubbery as they pull away from his fingers. I stand carefully, hugging myself tightly. I walk out the door, trying to get out of this murder house as quickly as possible.

"I will see you tomorrow, Birdie," The doctor calls after me. I stop with my hand on the door handle, my hand still trembling from a perfect mixture of pain and fear.

"I can change my own dressings," I offer, trying to sound as polite as possible, but it comes out as a garbled mess with me dripping blood down my chin. I don't want him touching me ever again. He grins at me, shaking his head, disagreeing with my words. "I will see you tomorrow, Birdie. It will be a big day for you, so get some rest," he says once more. His cold and calculating eyes fill me with horror, and one thing I know for sure is that I won't be getting any sleep tonight.

Robin meets me outside. She is sitting on the bottom concrete step and jumps up, looking relieved to see me.

"I have to take you back to the barn, I am told." I nod at her while wiping my chin on my white sleeves. Robin looks sullen when she understands why I am silent, with blood coming from my mouth. We walk in silence, back through the center of the village where everyone is working and down through the back where the large timber barn comes into view. The faded, stressed timber is like a castle to me. A sanctuary I never knew two days ago I would be thankful for. The soft banging of hammers and squeaky wheels from small wheelbarrows is distant behind us. While the village is steady with activity, I crave isolation.

"I miss Luca," I say in a mumble, more to myself, but as soon as I speak the words out loud, I regret them. Robin rubs the tops of her arms as a shiver runs through her.

"You really shouldn't say that. It will anger Axel and father." We walk through the dusty barn floor. I cringe at my feet. I never did get that wash. Robin catches my gaze and bites her bottom lip.

"I think someone is bringing you washing up stuff later, including shoes. You are oddly different, sister. They punish you severely, yet also let you get away with things we can not. If we leave our premises without shoes, we will have our feet whipped."

I nod slightly, understanding what she is saying. I guess they may feel sorry for me in some ways and, in other ways, jealous and wonder why I am getting treated differently. I wish she could see that I would give anything to not be here at all. Surely, she knows I am not here of my own free will. I walk into my room and gingerly sit on the edge of my bed, waiting for her to close the door. She hesitates, her mouth working but no words come out at first.

"Please don't cause trouble for Luca. We need him, Birdie," she tells me quietly.

"Why?"

"We just do. I shouldn't have said anything," she says, leaving me alone in the room.

I sit on my small cot for endless hours. The temperature in the room drops, so I know it is coming into nighttime now. The outside bolt wriggles and groans, then the small child from earlier walks in with a gown folded and draped over her shoulder and a tray of food carefully carried in her small grasp, sandals loosely hooked on two of her fingers. I bolt upright and take the shoes from her hands, trying to ease her load. I grab the tray from her hands and sit it gently on the floor. She steps backward out of the room, stretches, and then drags in a tin pail with steaming water and a washcloth. She grabs a towel, brings it back in, and places it at the foot of my bed. Making her way to the door, she holds the handle, ready to close me back in, but sneaks a curious glance at me. Her eyes bore into mine, but I don't feel anger or judgment. Just curiosity. I want to thank her. I want to apologize to her for having to act like my slave because those cunt men think they are somehow above anyone that has a vagina. But my tongue has swelled dangerously since I have been sitting in my isolated room, and I don't know how I will eat, let alone speak. I drop my eyes, avoiding her stare like a coward. I can't help her or myself, and I can't even fucking thank her. I hear the door slide shut, and I punch the cot beneath me. Every direction I look, every idea I have feels like a dead end. I am at a standstill. Helpless like a lamb being dragged to the slaughter. The thought of just ending it crosses my mind, but as I glance around the small room, I realize I don't even have a rope to make a noose, and the weak, tattered blanket under me would likely snap under my weight. I slide off the bed and crawl to the tray of food. My body feels weak all of a sudden, exhaustion and a come down from all the adrenaline that has been coursing through my veins, now leaving me depleted. I force myself to drink the glass of water, grimacing when it struggles to get past my raw, fat tongue. I pour a little water over my vegetable mash and mix it with a fork to make it smoother. I scoop it into my mouth the best I can with only a fork and swallow it down. The grilled red meat beside it looks good and smells even better, but I push the tray against the closed door. There's no way I could eat that. I grab the cloth from the hot water, run it over my face a few times, then slip it up my gown and wash the front of myself. I rinse my hands before finally dipping my feet to rinse them off. My toe stings, but I deal with it. I am learning what it truly means by physical pain is a state of mind. I wonder if any physical hurt I go through now will just be like a background hum in my life. I crawl back to my bed and huddle under the blanket so I am wrapped in it like a cocoon. Squeezing my eyes shut, I tell myself this isn't my life. I don't know how, but there will be a way for me to get away from here. Maybe I will save the little girl who looks at me with intelligent eyes that seek a life beyond this place.

The next morning, as I slip into a fresh gown, I can hear deep male voices booming through the barn. I eye the door warily because every time I am greeted by multiple males, it usually means I am also greeted with lashings or fucked up chores. I muse back to my earlier thoughts when laying on the cot wide awake and how I always had a life following my own strict routines. It's just how I navigated anxiety and made myself feel like I had my shit together. I wondered to myself if it was subconscious memories from this place that had me thinking that way or if I just have a weird OCD. I also had a crazed chuckle that I have well and truly skipped hair wash day, and my hair feels like a tangled bird's nest made from straw. My eyes snap up as the door opens, and they land directly on Axel and my father with a few others behind them. This is troublesome. I can feel it. Their energy is tense, and to bring it back up means I won't like whatever they are about to tell me.

"Good morning, Birdie. Today is a big day," Axel tells me, overly pleased. I say nothing. My tongue is enormous and the coppery tang taints my mouth, letting me know it's still actively bleeding.

"Come on, daughter, it is time to go to the doctor."

"Why," I carefully push the words through my rounded lips.

"You will finally be getting made back to how you should have stayed for me!" Axel says gleefully, making me more nervous and scared than if he spoke in anger. My head swivels between them as I try to figure out what is happening. I try to speak, but a choking sound comes out not only from my tongue but from the panic attack that's gripping my throat and squeezing the life out of my lungs. Axel straps forward and squeezes my jaw in his large hands, frowning deeply as he forces my mouth open with his painful grip.

"No wonder you are quiet for once." He sneers in my face and then talks to my father over his shoulder, "She has bitten her tongue nearly in half. It better be healed before the ceremony. I want her perfect." he bites out and then turns his head back to me. Strands of brown hair cover his inhuman eyes as his head is angled down to loom over me.

"The doctor will make you pure again today. Well, it's the best he can do for someone who has sinned severely. But you were chosen for me, and only me and you will be the only woman I have as my own! I will only take you as a virgin for our ceremony night, and by then, maybe you will know your place and learn to shut your mouth," his scolding voice dominates my attention. The words he is spewing out of his mouth finally sink in. The doctor. Virginity. Making me pure again. I try to back away from him, but his large hand is still wrapped around my jaw. His fingers are digging in so fiercely that my bones feel as if they may crumble under the pressure.

"Are you going to walk, or shall I drag you?" Axel threatens me. One moment, he talks to me calmly, like a saint who wants an equally angelic wife. Then, at other times, he fills me with terror, and I wonder if he is a sadist and all the men worship the devil in secret. I shake my head, "No," the mumbled word gets half stuck on my tongue. I sound like a baby.

"Oh yes," he says and picks me up, throwing me over his shoulder.

"Be careful with her," my father says with slight concern. It's the most emotion I have seen from him yet. My father shuffles behind, following us with his hands at his front. I start thrashing my fists against Axel's back and wailing loudly.

"You can't do thith." The S, in my words, is nonexistent right now.

"You boilet little brat, that'th what you are! A boilet stupid, whiny brat!"

"You better hope your tongue is healed the night of our ceremony, or you will bleed all over my cock when I make you suck it in front of everyone,"

"Axel, you can't speak to her like that. Remember where you are!" My father's voice comes from behind us between puffs. Axel is walking quickly toward the doctor's office, but all I can see is his back. I have given up punching. What's the point? Instead, as tears stream down my cheeks, I picture stab wounds all through Axel's back! *I will get him one day.* Because there is no way in hell, I will be sucking any part of his cock. I can't believe I have even tasted his cum. That moment of erotic weakness back in Coastal Town is now an image that makes me want to vomit. I hear doors open, followed by hushed male voices, so I know where we are now.

Axel drops me on the bed, the same one I was on yesterday, and I start screaming while I roll off the bed. The scream comes out as a gagging sound while I crumple on the floor in a heap. Making his way around the bed like an angry storm cloud chasing me, Axel stomps to me, where I watch with eyes like saucers. I scurry backward, pulling at my wounds as I roughly slide, but he is too quick for me. His hand wraps around my ankle, and he rips me towards him. I feel the wounds on my behind start bleeding again from the aggressive pull. He lifts me again, slamming me down on the bed.

"Stop fighting this, or I will tie you down and make him do it while you are wide awake." I spit in his face the best I can. Blood splatters over his nose, and I laugh when his face turns up in disgust. I cling to his white, flowy top, scratching and clawing as much as I can. My hair flies all around as my assault amps up.

"Luca will thave me!" I yell at him, knowing full well that I'm saying words that will send him into a wild frenzy. I get him hook, line, and sinker. He leans down, placing his elbow across my chest so I can't move. My hair is now tangled over my face, and loose strands caught on my tongue.

"Don't worry, I will make Luca watch as I fuck every hole you have!" he snarls, all riled up, before slapping me across the face.

"Axel, you need to remove yourself. She is still my daughter,"

"Yeah, and a couple more weeks until the ceremony, and then she will be mine, and I will be next in line to run this place. What I say, when it comes to her, still goes." He says across the bed to my angry-looking father. I'm not naïve, I think to myself as I breathe heavily, squinting to see him through my tousled hair. My father doesn't give a fuck about me. He doesn't like seeing the perfect cult he has created falling apart by the likes of us. Still leaning across my chest, Axel looks around the bed and uses his other hand to lift the brown leather straps. He fastens them around my wrists first. I start kicking my legs, but by the time he has strapped across my stomach, it is pointless. Axel comes to the foot of the bed, ignoring my kicking feet as if it is child's play, pulls apart leg stirrups at the base of the bed, and then straps my feet so they are bent at the knee and spread open.

"Everyone, get out now while the doctor works," Axel tells the room. Father gives him a questioning expression, but Axel only shakes his head.

"No, I will stay and ensure it is done correctly."

"Fuck off, Axel," I yell at him. He moves to the head of the bed once more to speak quietly in my ear,

"I would be quiet if I were you, or I will stuff a cloth in your mouth, and with the already swollen tongue, you may not make it out alive." He stands back up straight but stays beside me. The doctor sits on a small black stool that has wheels on it and wheels himself so he is positioned perfectly between my legs. There is no dignity, and it's invasive. He snips at my panties so they fall apart in the middle.

"She stays awake for her little performance," Axel snides loudly. I'm flat on my back, so I can't see much now, but if I know the sick old man, I bet he is grinning ear to ear.

"I will give you a local, so you shouldn't feel anything, Birdie," The doctor tells me like a true professional.

"Do you want me to stitch her lips together? I can't concentrate while she is being so loud," his old gravelly voice says so casually I wonder if I heard right. Have they finally broken me completely? Because I stay silent as I stare at the ceiling with tears streaming down my cheeks, down onto the bed. I never knew eyes could produce so much salty liquid until I came here.

"I will be quiet," I nearly whisper.

"Good," the doctor says, and I swear I could feel his horrendous hot breath on my lady parts. I make the mistake of sliding my eyes across to Axel, staring between my legs with a smile so big you would almost think he had won the lottery. Maybe in his fucked up head, he thinks he has? I feel a sharp pinch and take a deep breath in. It's followed by another deep pinching feeling, so I assume it's the local getting put in. The needle pricks sting badly when he injects it deeper inside of me. Axel and the Doctor talk quietly for a few minutes about the work that must be done before winter as if it's just another day. My hair is tickling my nose, but I refuse to ask Axel to push the remaining strands away from my face. Instead, I close my eyes and start counting in my head, calming myself as much as possible.

1, 2, 3, 4, 5—I feel a tugging and pushing on my vagina wall. A loud clicking sound and more pushing remind me of the pap smear tests I have had. My natural reaction has me tensing my thighs, wanting to try and slam them shut. The thought of the doctor happily stitching my mouth closed keeps me from following through on my human instincts. I feel some slight pinching and a lot of movement deeper inside me. I let out a long breath through my nose. 6, 7, 8, 9, 10, 11, 12. I keep counting, ignoring the chit-chat and poking and prodding. I get to 2043 before the doctor stands up, rips off one glove, and places a hand on my bare knee. He rests on it while he chats to Axel.

"I have done the best I can with what was there. With her age and sexual history, I had to create a whole new hymen, cutting at other bits and connecting them in the appropriate place. All the best for the ceremony night, Axel," the doctor informs him with a toothy smile like Axel deserves congratulations for what has just happened to me.

"Thanks, Doctor. I am looking forward to it." He nods, stretching his arms over his head. He brings his arms back down to stroke my forehead.

"Birdie, the local will last another hour, maybe at best. After that, you will be very sore. Don't do anything too physical, or you will tear the stitches, and we will have to do this again. And there is always the possibility of stitching the opening closed until ceremony day, so don't do anything stupid. I have put a pad in your underwear as there will be some bleeding." his matter-of-fact voice says before then he leaves the room. Axel walks around, undoing all the bindings before reaching his hand under my elbow to sit me up.

"Let's go. You need to eat," he says so close to my ear that I feel strands of my hair bounce from the movement. I thought I knew hatred before. I thought I knew what being broken was. This is different. Axel tenses beside me as he tugs me toward the door to leave.

"Are you going to start behaving Birdie? I never know what to think when you are silent. With you, it could be good or utterly bad." I narrow my gaze as the common area comes into view and see large groups of families entering. He has forgotten about my tongue, the stupid loser. I stop, coming to an abrupt halt, my elbow throbbing from Axel's hold still on it. He nearly snaps it off when he doesn't realize I have stopped. I spit down onto his feet, and bubbly, red saliva pools on his shoes. I look back up to his face, shrugging my shoulders at him innocently.

"You will fucking pay for that," he says before kicking my feet out from under me, making me land in a heap at his ankles. I land on my side, but it doesn't stop my arse from hurting.

"Should I make you lick it off, Birdie? Is that it? You want to eat up the mess you have created!?" He roars at me. I slowly push myself onto my hands and knees, then crane my neck so we are eye to eye again.

"Wipe it off with your sleeve, you animal! You can find some broth to eat and then get yourself cleaned up!" I slap my wrist down onto his feet and wipe the bloody spit off. The entire time, I am thinking up creative ways I can behead him. The farm equipment in the barn could make it fun.

What's that saying about the snowball effect? I think that is what is happening in my life. Getting my hymen sewn back into place yesterday was rock bottom and soul destroying. It's an intimate type of betrayal. The pain all night has been horrific. As soon as the local wore off, I was left with cramping, stinging, and pinching in my vagina and deep within my stomach. But now I perch on my makeshift toilet while tears roll down my cheeks. There's too much blood. I've had a small amount of bleeding overnight in my sanitary pad, but now I glance between my thighs and see the fresh red blood in the bucket along with my bloated stomach, and I know it's my period. Luca's words are flashing like neon lights in my mind. *They will wait until you have had a full cycle.* I have no way of hiding this from them. With this fresh blood, the ceremony or rape, as I would call it, looms closer. I step off the bucket, eyes growing wide as the door rattles and the small girl tiptoes in again, carrying my breakfast. Her eyes flick between me and the bucket, catching the fresh droplets of blood on the ground. She steps back, looking regretful but on a mission. I lurch forward and grab onto her wrist.

"Please don't tell them. Help me clean it up. They will never have to know. Please," I beg her. Begging a small child leaves me feeling ill, but with limited options, I shamelessly plead with her again. Giving me one last sullen look, she pulls her hand out of my grip and takes off running. Becoming frantic and losing grip on reality, I grab my blanket off my bed. I throw it over the beam above me before my eyes crawl around the room until they land on a bucket. I flip the bucket up, not even batting an eyelid at the urine and blood that pours out. Standing on the bucket now, I tie the blanket firmly around the beam, ready to be done with this. I can only hope this blanket won't snap before the job is done. They have already taken my dignity and sanity. They will get nothing more from me. I start wrapping the blanket around my neck when Axel comes rushing in. His eyes widen with shock when he understands what I am trying to do.

"You stupid girl!" He screams, voice ripping through the large barn. He charges at me and pulls me off the bucket. I sob uncontrollably. All I needed was one more minute, and this nightmare would have been ended. Axel holds me against his body, sneering down into my face.

"You're coming with me. You thought your life was bad before? I will show you what bad is. I have tried to be nice." Axel hisses against my hair as he carries me out, almost like I am a baby. I try to kick my legs, but he is too strong for me and has me folded nearly in half against his chest. He charges through the barn, right down to the back of it. The back of the barn I haven't ventured into yet. He boots open a door that swings into a small cubicle-like space. No windows and no lights on the ceiling. The musty smell makes my nose wrinkle, and I try to shy my head away from the sight.

"No, no, no, no, no," I chant over and over again. Not this. Not darkness. He drops me on the ground, and I cry out as pain shoots up through my vagina.

"Oh yes." He says down at my crumpled body on the dirt ground. His hand snakes out behind the door and drops a bowl of oats on the ground.

"Eat it." He says and slams the door shut. I bang on the door, desperate to be let out. It's no use, though, as I hear his heavy footsteps getting farther and farther away. I bring my knees up to my chin, hugging myself tightly. My eyes scan around me, but there is nothing but darkness and a damp, earthy smell. *Someone by now must be coming for me? Any day now someone will bust through this place with the police, and they will save me. I hope.*

I lay my head on my knees and close my eyes. I start counting in my head. Endlessly. Every time my mind begins to shut off and I lose count, I start again. Time takes on a whole new meaning. A meaning where time actually means nothing at all. Minutes don't matter. Hours drift by, turning into days. I barely notice when the door creaks open every now and then, with a bowl of food getting slid across the dirt toward me. Then, the door closes once more, and I am blanketed in utter darkness again. I don't know how much time has passed exactly, but my period is easing up now. Maybe three days, then? Who really knows. Because it doesn't make a difference. My once wet, fresh blood has dried on me, and time still creeps on. I rock and count. Rock and count. The door opens, and food and water are pushed in. Door closed. Darkness and cold consume me again. I rock and count. Rock and count. My cheeks have long dried. No tears are left in my body. My back aches, and my head throbs from being stuck in this position for so long. But I keep rocking back and forth on my behind. The soft tickle of cockroaches running over my feet is nothing to me now. The door creaks open again, but the small child who provides food isn't in the light. It's Axel. There are multiple women behind him, and I realize what today is. Has that much time really passed already?

"You stink and look like shit. You will go with the women to bathe and prepare for the ceremony tonight. Get up," he orders me. I try. I really do because why fight it? But my limbs feel as if they are cemented down, and I am paralyzed. Axel steps in, cringing when he gets closer to me and grips me under my armpits. He lifts me to my feet, and my pelvis trembles when I try to put weight on my legs.

"Help her," he yells at the women. "I don't want to touch her again until she is cleaned up," he continues saying as he walks past them. His shoulders knock one of them sideways, leaving her to rub her shoulder. She shuffles into the doorway with a submissive posture and stands on one side of me. Her black curly hair covers my shoulder as she and the other female put their arms around me. I shuffle slowly, looking straight ahead. The light hurts my eyes, and my eyelids fight me. I want to close them against the burning, but I force them open as much as I can. I stumble alongside my helpers, and they take me into a small house. The living room and kitchen are small and open-plan. A small door off it holds a single tub filled with already steaming water.

"I can do the rest," I tell them. They share questioning looks between them, like a silent conversation.

"I can climb into the tub myself," I assure them once more. They agree silently by dipping their heads with their hands wrapped behind their backs. I slip off my underwear and tug the gown over my head before lifting my leg, climbing into the tub, and sinking under the water. I submerge my head and scrub my hair and face with my hands. As I re-emerge and take a deep breath, I feel the worried faces of the women in the doorway. Word from my desperate attempts at ending this nightmare has spread, obviously. The now red, murky water floats around me, and I sigh heavily.

"There are things out there worse than death, you know?" I say quietly as I soak in the warm water. They give each other a soft nod before they creep into the bathroom. The one with black curly hair pushes her hand straight into the water, causing me to jump back from the shock. I shut my legs tightly and cover my breasts with my arms, then screech, "What are you doing?" The usually serious face morphs into a smile. She actually smiles and rips the plug out. As the water drains, the other woman pours a bucket of hot water over me and turns the cold tap on. They both kneel beside the bath now.

"Do you really get to speak freely where you come from?" One asks hesitantly. Her voice is so soft and quiet. I stare into her light hazel eyes and sigh. The golden hues remind me of the beach. I start to relax, almost comforted by the fact I'm being let into a secret girls club.

"Yeah. It's crazy that you talk about it like I have come from an alien world. Have no outsiders ever found this place?"

The other one talks in a hushed tone, "Yeah, a few times, but the men say they are the evil ones trying to destroy our ways, and they get sacrificed,"

"What do you mean by sacrifice?" I need to learn to shut my mouth because sometimes ignorance is bliss.

"They are fed to the crows."

"Have you ever thought about trying to overpower them and leave?"

"One woman tried to leave a long time ago and got caught. Your mom is the only one who could ever get out."

"The women hate you but admire you at the same time for that."

"Why are you talking to me now? I know you are scared you will get in trouble." The one with the yellow eyes answers first.

"Because we know there is no way out for you now. We don't want you to feel alone." I sniff in, trying to hold in a sob.

"What's the ceremony like?" I ask.

"If you lay really still, it's not so bad. If you fight, it will be harder for you and more painful." The one with brown eyes says and turns the tap off. They get up and leave me there to finish washing myself. Once I have climbed out and dressed into a new gown, they tell me to sit in a small chair. They dry my hair for me, brush it for a long time, and then create a long braid down my back. They hand me a small mirror and press it into my trembling fingers. I don't look immediately. I haven't looked in a mirror since I lived in Coastal Town. I don't know where to go from here. *Do I give up? Do I keep fighting?* I gingerly lift the mirror, take a deep, steadying breath, and then stare at the girl looking back. I gasp before I chew the inside of my cheek. It's me, but not me at all. My fingers lightly trace the small hollows under my eyes that now appear too big for my face, and I run a finger over my lips, which are dry and slightly cracked from the dehydration. One of the women notices my movements and brings me some Vaseline. She slides it over my lips and gives me an encouraging expression.

"What is your name?" I whisper to her. Her mouth opens as she prepares to answer, then jumps back when there's a loud knock at the door. Axel stomps in then his eyes take in my appearance, more pleased this time. He has his hands stretched up to the top of the door frame as he appreciates the view. "It's time," he announces with pride before stepping back out. Nothing more is spoken from him. He is disconnected from reality, focusing solely on having me as his prized trophy. The women lead me out to the meadow; we say nothing. I glance at the forest across the clearing, contemplating trying my luck at running into it and escaping. It is just the field of lilies between me and the dense bush. But a moment later, as if robotic, I find myself walking down the long pathway. The men are lined up on either side of the path again before the entrance, all wearing their crow's heads.

"You, chosen ones, are dismissed," my father proclaims, making the women rush away.

"Come on, Birdie," he orders me. I follow him into the room. Remembering what the girls said. If I just lie still, it will be over before I know it.

"Lay down on the ceremony bed," he says, and I climb onto it. Lying on my back, I stare at the ceiling. The room fills with the men. They stand around the perimeter, and heavy footsteps enter the small hut. Axel.

Axel climbs onto the slab, hovering over my body and holding himself up by his arms. He is topless now, causing me to grimace. My eyes rake over his body again because I refuse to meet his eyes. His body feels warm. So warm that I almost want to huddle closer to it. I don't like the things my body is telling me. The man above me deserves to die slowly and painfully. Axel's body quivers over me, and I let my eyes drift lower until they fall on the bulge in his white linen pants. It's massive, threatening to break through his pants. I suck on my bottom lip, feeling myself becoming heated. Maybe I have a sick kink of enjoying being watched because this was seriously fucked up on too many levels. My eyes trail back up, following every straining muscle and ripple on his firm torso. They drift over his neck full lips, along the perfectly chiseled jaw bone, and then land on his eyes. Our eyes are locked. Unable to move from each other. The eyes that paralyze me and take my words away. These eyes don't belong to Axel at all.

"I'm sorry," he says so quietly it's almost just a soft breath across my face. Luca cages me in my place, his forearms on either side of my head. His thumbs brush against my forehead gently, soothing me. I'm at a loss for words. In a situation like this, what would ever suffice?

"I'm glad it's you," I whisper back. I knew he would save me. I just didn't know how. He slides his fingers down my chiffon gown, making it feel like butterflies fluttering across my stomach. Two fingers slide down into my panties, rubbing gently between my crease, seeking my nub. When they find my small beaded g-spot between my two lips, he starts caressing in small circles. Gentle touches under his strained arms make me realize he is holding back. He is being gentle for me, but it is a battle within himself not to be forceful. Luca scares me, but as a contradiction, I also trust him more than anyone in this room. I trust him with my life. My body responds to him because he owns my body. I've known it since the first day we met. No matter the situation, my body will never not be a slave to Luca's every need and want. His fingers glide over my wetness and back up over my clit. My chest rises as I succumb to the desires running through my body. I don't know what Luca is feeling at this moment. Triumph? Fear? Satisfaction? Either way, his eyes widen when he feels how wet I am for him, how ready I am to please him. His lips part as a hungry whoosh of breath flows out. Whatever he was holding back from me is gone. It feels like there is no one in the room anymore, the surrounding chaos has disappeared, and it is just us two caught up in the throws of sexual need.

"My Birdie," He breathes against my face. He then removes his fingers from my pussy and positions himself against my opening. His hard cock nudges against my entrance, begging, no, demanding to be let in. I relax my legs so my thighs fall further apart, and he groans in satisfaction. His hips thrust forward, and his hard cock pushes into my pussy like a puzzle piece, finally finding its home. I cry out as my freshly repaired hymen is shredded once more. He moves quicker as if my pain is fueling his attack on me. He is marking me, claiming me as his own. He moves faster, leaning down on one elbow and his other hand teasing my nipple through my gown. I find myself solely focused on his hard chest that has a sheen of sweat over it above my head. My hips raise to his rhythm; the sharp pain within me is pushing my desire to force him deeper. I want him to completely destroy what the doctor and Axel did to me. This is a revenge I never knew I needed. My muscles clench tightly as I feel my orgasm cresting. I moan, and Luca leans down, swallowing it with an overbearing kiss. His tongue pushes into my mouth, massaging my near-healed tongue. He pulls away, leans his forehead against mine, and whispers the words

"He never deserved you. Neither do I. But if it's between me or him that you have to be stuck with. It'll always be me." He pushes into me deeply one last time, my hips raising high until his shaft rubs along my G-spot, and our releases meet each other. My muscles clenching tightly, massage his cock, milking the last of his cum. Luca pulls out of me slowly as if remembering where we are and begins to act cautious.

"I will take my chosen one to my quarters now," his deep voice commands everyone's attention. I slowly sit up, hugging myself, too scared to see any gazes. How can they not tell it's Luca. "You did well, Axel. May the gods bless us with a new child from the chosen," my father says, clapping him on the shoulder before leaving. Everyone follows my father, clapping him on the shoulder in the same congratulatory way. I should be angry at them. But I'm still stunned by what just went down.

"Let's go," Luca growls in my direction, holding his hand to me. He helps me off the concrete slab and pulls me along impatiently.

"We need to talk," I say in a hushed voice behind him.

"Later," he snaps back, my man of not many words back to feeling himself. We walk for a few minutes as he rushes me through the village and back to the house I bathed in. It dawns on me this must be Axel's house.

"Where is Axel?" I say as he propels me into the lounge and slams the door shut. He spins, staring at me like a stalker with his prey in sight. My breath hitches when his broody eyes slide over my body and linger on my puckered nipples that I know are visible through the thin material.

"I thought I could handle it,"

"Handle what?" I say, watching Luca creep closer to me. But I'm not scared. My body feels electric.

"I tried to be good. I tried to bide my time, but when I found out the ceremony would be tonight, I had to get back. I was nearly too late. I would have slaughtered him had he touched you," as the last words leave his parted lips, he has reached me. He snakes a hand around my waist and pulls me to him roughly.

"Where is Axel?" I ask again.

"Later," he growls and attacks my mouth with his so savagely I feel my small cracks burst open. But lost in the moment, I ignored it. I wrap my arms around his neck, pulling him even closer like I need to wear him as a second skin. He pulls back, breaking our kiss, and then raps both his large hands around the collar of my thin gown. While staring at me with hooded eyes, he grits his teeth and rips the dress straight down the middle, so I am completely exposed. He traces his bottom lip with his tongue, breathing so loudly that it almost echoes through the modest house. "Get on your knees," he orders roughly. I hesitate briefly, which angers him.

"Don't do that. When it's you and I, there is no room for being fucking shy. You're all mine, and you will do as you are told. Get. On. Your. Fucking. Knees," he bites out.

I drop to my knees, his overly tall body casting a shadow over me.

"Does it feel good doing as you are told?" he asks, tilting his head as his dominating gaze is forced upon me. "Yes," I answer honestly. Oh, this feels good. It shouldn't, and I know that. But it does.

"You don't have a submissive bone in your body. You defy everyone and fight back. But with me," he pauses and strokes the top of my head, "You obey every fucking order. I'll kill for you, Birdie, and I will happily die for you. But you will obey every word that comes out of my mouth while I still breathe. Now wrap your hands around my cock and suck my fucking dick," he growls low and steadily. I crawl closer to him. He growls when I shyly look up at him through my long lashes, my braid hanging loosely over my shoulder.

"Like my own fucking angel. Too bad the things I want to do to you are anything but angelic." He tugs his waistband down, lowering his pants, and his hard cock springs free. A large ripple of veins runs through it, and I can't decide if it is angry or excited. Either way, my mouth waters, and my excited juices smear on the inside of my thighs along with his earlier pleasures. My trembling fingers wrap around the base of his shaft, and I turn my head up slightly, taking one of his balls into my mouth.

"Oh, Birdie, my little expert," he murmurs as I massage his nut with my tongue. After I let the ball slide out of my mouth, I trail my tongue over his other one and then up the long, hard length. His balls tighten, and a shudder runs through his toned thighs. I use one hand to steady myself against his thigh, and with the other still gripping his impressive cock, I take it into my mouth. I take the whole length until it rams the back of my throat, and I gag. I slowly slide it back out of my mouth. I tease the end of it, running my tongue around his head before taking it into my mouth once more, and then skim my lips over the shaft. I massage his cock with my tongue as my mouth glides up and down. I can already taste the saltiness in my mouth, so I know he is close. I move my mouth up and down faster and squeeze the base with my hand. I usually wouldn't, but Luca is different. I can see a depraved man in him. I pull my mouth away and run my hand firmly up and down his shaft, pumping it rapidly. It twitches under my grip, and more pre cum dribbles out of the end. It catches on my hand and then slides down his cock as I move my hand back down in long strokes.

"Nah, you are drinking this one, Birdie," Luca bites out before he grips my braid painfully, wraps it around his fist, and forces my mouth back over his cock. He fucks my mouth a few times, slamming it in as far as he can each time.

"Fuck..." he grinds out, and then cum fills the back of my throat. I swallow it down as his cock spasms in my mouth and against my tongue.

We lay on the small couch afterward. Well, I am lying; he is caging me in with his large frame over the top of me. He nibbles the bottom of my ear and then nuzzles my neck before pressing kisses along my collarbone.

"Are you going to tell me where your brother is?" I ask, deciding what I want more, answers or Luca to ignore my question and keep working his way down my body. Luca tenses at my question but doesn't stop. I sigh loudly, more to myself because I am about to ruin this moment, but I need answers. I place my hands on either side of his head and pull at it so he has to face me. I arch an eyebrow at him in question while I wait for the answer.

"You are gonna give me fucking blue balls now."

"Okay, firstly, how when you have emptied them twice? And secondly, I need to know."

"Firstly, it doesn't matter how many times I cum; when I am around you, I have blue balls, and they feel heavy," he says in a mocking tone. "And secondly, I want to spend at least twenty-four hours exploring your body all to myself before we have to talk about my brother," he says with brows furrowing in the middle. I don't answer; I just wait for him to tell me.

"Look, I heard the ceremony was today, so I rushed back as fast as I could. I was terrified I wouldn't make it in time. No one, ever, can touch you. I won't allow it. I went into a frenzy, knocked Axel out, and now he's in the pit. I haven't figured out what to do with him yet." I sit up on my elbows because that's all Luca's body will allow, and think over what he has just said. "What's the pit?"

"A small dark room with no windows. It's in the back of the barn. A place I will never wish upon you," he says softly now, going from beast to sympathetic. I bite my lip. He doesn't know.

"Luca, I was in there. Today's my first day out since I tried to hang myself," I admit to him. It feels like a lifetime ago now. His reaction is not what I expected, though. The beast is back. My jaw explodes in pain as he grips me harshly. The tips of his fingers press into my skin painfully. "What do you mean you tried to hang yourself?" he growls into my face. Our noses are nearly touching, and unable to turn my head, I am forced to meet his furious eyes, searching mine as if I have betrayed him.

"Don't look at me like that. You weren't here."

"You tried to take yourself away from me? You were going to leave me?" he growls, betrayal whipping his words at me. My body goes cold like ice.

"I wasn't thinking of you! I had tunnel vision. All I could see was Axel raping me. You have no idea what I went through while you were gone." I sniff, then continue, "Turns out there are things worse than death anyway. Like being locked in the pit for weeks!"

"I don't know whether I should lock you away so you don't try to leave me again or kill Axel and everyone else here right now for putting you in there!"

"He's evil. I have never got good vibes from him." I mumble quietly, trying not to let on that the fucked up idea of Luca locking me up is turning me on. Luca climbs off me but never breaks our touch. He pulls me onto him and sits on the couch so I am now straddling him. He throws me around like I am a feather. I guess I am to him.

"Did your mom ever talk about this place and why she ran away?" he asks me, seriously, with those searching eyes studying me.

"Nope, she never spoke on who my father was or where we came from."

"I may have only been four, but I still remember. I wish I didn't, but I do. You were always promised to be with Axel. As soon as you were born. But he was always not right in the head. He was always hidden away, mutilating small creatures and being heavy-handed with the girls. Especially you because he knew in some sort of way, he already owned you," Luca says as he traces my lips with his finger and then trails his hand down my back so it's resting on the slight curve.

"One day, you tripped over on the stones, and I picked you off the ground and helped brush the stones off your grazed knee. I was always following you around, making sure you were okay. Then Axel saw me and started throwing a tantrum. He kept screaming 'mine, mine, mine' over and over again. He took off running and hid away for hours. By the time he came back, he was carrying a dead crow with its head missing, and he dumped it on your dinner plate when everyone was seated. After that, I think your mom decided she wouldn't let you be with someone like him, so she ran away with you. She also knew that you being Axel's chosen one meant he would run this place one day, and that scared all the women."

"How the fuck did he get away with that?"

"It is the way it has always been. Although I'm sure you have noticed that," Luca says, then falls silent. I watch him work his jaw, and worry takes hold of his features.

"Every day I woke up, wondering if they would have found you and your mom. You were the highlight of every day for me. You were like this happy, innocent little angel running around and I wanted to be with you every moment I could. But you never returned. I never forgot about you though. Your features slowly faded from my mind as I got older. Time makes us forget some things. But the feeling I had back then never faded. I guess you were my light in the darkness. Without you, all I had was darkness. I wasn't allowed to go to school since I never had any reason to learn of the ceremonies and rules with our chosen ones. I was always just made to hangout and occupy myself until I got old enough to do more physical things."

"I am so sorry you had to go through that. Maybe someone from Coastal will find us? Someone will know I am missing by now."

"I don't think anyone will come looking for you Birdie." He says sadly.

"Why?"

"When I left for business, it was to make sure no one was going to come looking for you. I left letters, message people off your cell phone that was left in the house. I made it look like you left to travel since your mom has gone now."

"Oh my god. So I am never getting out of this." I feel so hurt, so angry. But also I understand he was made to do it. You always think, if you were ever in a situation like this you would run and take any chance you got to get away. But when you are in the situation, you are beaten down so badly that you think there is no getting out so the fight in you disappears.

"I was hoping we wouldn't find you, you know. Although you have always crossed my mind, wondering where you were and what you were doing. But we did find you, and when we were sent to bring you back, I told myself I would ignore you because you weren't worth messing up my plans. And then I saw you again in the café. Still the most beautiful person on this planet. And then you opened your fiery mouth, and I knew I would have to find a way to change the plan so I could stop you from getting hurt."

"What plan?" I ask, wondering what on earth he is talking about. These are the most words he has ever spoken to me, yet he still makes no sense. He chuckles quietly, and I watch his chest shake. I run a finger lightly across his abs, and goosebumps erupt over his bare skin. His hand moves quickly, snatching my hand in his to stop the subtle movements. He brings it to his mouth and kisses my palm before placing it back on his chest.

"A friend of mine and I have been working for years, trying to find a way to get everyone out safely. Well, the ones that want to go. Some truly believe this is the better way of life. It's a long game plan. We have been skimming one or two rifles from the collection here and there over the last few years and stashing money when we know no one will notice a little missing. We can't just over power them. But now I need to speed things up because how long can I keep Axel in the pit without someone finding him?"

"Just kill him!" I suggest quickly, but Luca's stricken look stops me, and I close my mouth.

"He's my twin brother, Birdie. Despite everything, it still feels like he is part of me."

"So how is this going to work then?"

"I honestly have no fucking idea. I have promised some of the kids I will save them, though, and now they look to me expectantly. You must stay in line for now, though, Birdie, and play the part. You have no idea what these men are capable of. I've seen each and every one of them turn into monsters with no redeeming qualities. I can't risk them hurting one of the kids because I challenge them."

"They would do that?" I ask, shocked. He lets go of my hand and pushes a strand of hair away from my face.

"They would, and they will. You haven't seen the worst of this place Birdie. They have weapons stored, poisons stashed away and they have, in the past, put poisons in the drinks of ones they think are betraying them. We want to get them all out safely. Not just rush it and get one or two out." Luca grips the back of my head and starts nuzzling my neck. His intentions clearly to move on from the heavy conversation.

"Wait, what's the little girl's name? The one that brings me food? She's one of them, isn't she?" He scoffs loudly, causing his breath to brush against my now-dampened neck.

"Last thing on my mind now is little kids, Birdie! Her name is Violet, okay? Now, if you don't mind, I have an issue that needs attention," he growls as he slips his hands down my body, lifts my gown, and tugs it up and over my head. I can feel his issue that needs attention. It's pressed firmly against my wet core, and it feels magical. He grinds his pelvis into my own, causing a soft friction.

"Is it sore?" he asks softly, breathing loudly between each word.

"A little, but it's okay," I answer, although he hears the uncertainty in my words.

"It's not okay. I only ever want you sore because I fucked you until your pussy is swollen and your thighs bruised after you have had endless orgasms. It's not okay that you're sore for any other reason. Go lay on the bed," he orders me. I clamber off him and find my way to the small twin bed beside the bathroom in the small square room. I lay on it. Completely naked and feeling a hot mixture of fear and excitement. My eyes lock with Luca's leaning on the door frame, arms crossed at his chest, and hungry eyes drinking me in. I'm his for the taking, and he knows it.

The lust is coming off me in waves. My breasts move up and down quickly as my breathing comes in fast increments. I can feel the hardness of my nipples, standing tall and almost becoming painful. My thighs rub together, and I almost whimper with intense need. My wetness has coated the inside of my thighs, and rubbing them together, feeling them glide over my slick need, is too much.

"Please," I say, no beg, Luca. He can do whatever he wants to me as long as it is now.

"Please, what, Birdie?" he asks as he pushes off the door frame and stalks closer to me. Every step is measured and calculated.

"Please pleasure me. Please give me the release my body so desperately needs." The bed lowers under his weight as he leans down onto it and then crawls on top of me.

"Do you want me pleasuring you or Axel, baby?" My body goes still under him when that name leaves his mouth.

"You..." I breathe, but my muscles clench tightly when I remember how I nearly had them both. *Sick, sick, sick. That is what I am.* But where I am now and what I have been through, I feel like the thoughts in my head are nothing compared to what really happens here. A smirk tugs at the corners of Luca's lips, and his mesmerizing eyes drill into mine.

"Are you sure? If my memory serves correctly, you didn't mind having the both of us, didn't you? You greedy girl," he murmurs, then drops his head and bites one of my nipples. My back arches, and the sudden jolt of pain I feel sends a quiver right through me. It hurt but also made me soak myself.

"If you could have us both, would you?"

"N-no," I stutter slightly and gasp when he bites the other nipple.

"Lies, Birdie. My greedy girl would take us both if we offered it. Maybe one day I'll tie him up on the bed for you. You can do what you like with him while I watch," he says and slides his fingers between my sensitive lips and pushes them inside me forcefully. He grins at me and watches my face as he slides two fingers in and out of my pussy.

"What I am feeling right now confirms everything I have said. My greedy, depraved girl." He pushes a third finger in, and I feel my muscles fight the motion, clamping around his hand. He pulls all three fingers out, sits back on his knees, and sucks them all. I sit up on my elbows, panting rapidly, and look at my red and purple nipples with teeth marks on them. My eyes slide down my body, and then I grab onto Luca. His ripped thighs are spread apart, and his long, thick erection is throbbing and beautiful against his stomach. My eyes trail up his torso and land on his cocky face. He shakes his head at me.

"Tsk, tsk, you don't get that yet, Birdie," he growls at me. Luca wraps both his arms around my thighs, sinks back, and then nestles himself between them. He doesn't start slowly. He dives straight in, knowing exactly what he wants. He buries his tongue deep inside me and groans. "Birdie?" he says once he has removed his tongue.

"Yeah?" I breathe, wanting him to put his tongue right back where it was. "I will save you from each and every one of them. But believe me when I say I will also be the one destroying you," he bites out, and his thick hot breath flows over my damp pussy. Without any more talking, he dives back in. Swirling his tongue deeply. I should care if his cum is still inside me from earlier, but if he doesn't care, then neither do I. He takes my nub into his mouth and sucks on the small ball of nerves. It sends my body into overdrive. I shamelessly raise my hips and rock them against his face. He grips my thighs harder and sends a long lick over my clit. He then swirls his tongue over it and flicks it with the tip of his tongue. It sends me soaring, and my pussy clenches over and over as my climax rips through my body with force. I moan loudly when the last shudder wracks through me. Luca crawls back up over me with wet, shiny lips. I watch him as he licks my juice off them, savoring every bit he can. He then rips the pillow out of the pillowcase and wraps it around my neck painfully. Not enough to suffocate me, but the pressure is leaving my skin burning. He positions his hips between mine, and his considerable length edges into my entrance. With one hand wrapped around the pillowcase, he lifts my head off the mattress so my back is angled painfully. His other hand grips under my arse, and I look into his satisfied face as he thrusts his thick cock into me painfully. I want to scream out, but the pillowcase is tight, cutting off my ability to make noise. I should be scared of these torturous ways. I should be quivering and crying in a corner somewhere. But somehow, my body was humming with energy. I become lightheaded when he thrusts in deeper. He is relentless, like a savage beast taking his fill. With one more hard dive into me, he groans loudly and drops me back down onto the bed. His hands slam down on either side of my face with his fingers spread wide and palms flat. He is heaving in breaths while sweat drips from his forehead onto my face. My head is still swimming, and as if the beast has been put back into its cage, he carefully unwraps the pillowcase from my neck, drops down beside me, and pulls me hard against his body. This is the safest I have ever felt in my life.

We both fall into a steady rhythm of breathing and as my eyes close, instead of having a nightmare of crows and monsters, I dream about a small boy with soft eyes comforting me when I am hurt.

"Birdie, it is time to wake up," I feel a warm, breathy sentence tickle my ear. I roll over to face Luca, and the pang of pain I feel between my legs reminds me of how quickly yesterday twisted and my once sealed fate had changed. Now, I see hope for a different future. I don't think it will still ever be the future I had always wanted, but now, with a tainted soul and fractured spirit, it's the future I can only see myself enjoying now. One with Luca, wherever that may be. I tuck myself into his chest and lay still, hoping he will tell me we can hibernate in this bed all day. His warm chest vibrates against my face, and then it is followed up with a soft sigh. I wait for what I know is coming.

"We have to keep up appearances, okay? I know you can do this, Birdie; otherwise, I would have admitted defeat already," he whispers, grips my cheek, and rubs his thumb over my lips so softly I could almost forget about the depraved fucking he gave me last night.

"You are the strongest woman I know. You got this," he assures me, and I snort, rolling out of his hold and off the bed.

"Luca, let's be honest, you don't know that many women to compare me to," As I find my gown again, he scoots across the bed and pulls me to him.

"Don't ever remove yourself from my hold ever again. Have you got that?" he scolds me.

"Sorry," I mumble. He's overbearing and possessive, but god, when he gets like this, I melt. I want him to look after me. I have been independent and strong for so long. But with Luca, I want to break and crumble around him, let him pick up the pieces and put me back together again. His being consumes me so much I think I would happily die if he ever tried to leave me. He is the anchor in my life now, keeping me from floating away into nothingness. Luca spins me around so I am straddling his thighs on the edge of the bed. I feel his acceptance of my apology pressing painfully against my core.

"I'm sore."

"I know I will be gentle. You're my drug of choice, Birdie, and I will happily embrace my fucking addiction." He moves his hips and rubs against my pussy. I feel the dull ache from bruises, but there is also the increasing pleasure tingling in my core. He keeps moving slowly while he stares into my eyes. It is almost unnerving but also so erotic. He is so gentle and slow that it doesn't take long for my wetness to start coating the length of his shaft as he runs it up and down, through my lips, and across my clit, then sliding back down so slowly. The hefty veins in his shaft create small ribbed patterns that increase the pleasure. With the last, painfully slow movement up my pussy and over my slick nub, Luca grips both my arse cheeks, lifts me high, and then pushes me down onto his cock until I am tight against the base and we are flush against each other. I whimper before grabbing onto his bare shoulders and digging my nails into them. I try to hold myself still, giving myself time to adjust to the thick intrusion inside of me. The aching inside me is painful. Luca is strong and relentless, though. Ignoring the blood now being drawn on his shoulders from my nails, he slides my hips up and back down, groaning loudly as his cock sinks deep within me again.

"Squeeze harder, baby. Make me bleed more. It'll just make me cum harder," he groans out. I do as he says, enjoying releasing some of my own hurt on someone. I feel the skin pop more under my nails as the small cuts open up wider and become deeper. Blood trickles down my long fingers. He pulls me up and down harder, faster, matching his deep, frequent groans now. Something inside me changes as the heat from his now sweaty torso rubs against my hard nipples. The pain inside my bruised pussy is being replaced by a building climax. Every stroke his cock makes against the G-spot inside of me, I moan along with him. The next long stroke does it, and I am quivering on top of Luca from the most incredible climax. He matches me, cumming at the same time and holding my pussy firmly against his cock as it spasms and releases cum deep inside me. Once we have caught our breaths again, he slowly lifts me off him, back to being gentle and loving.

"Wait here, I will quickly run you a bath to wash you off, and then we can go for breakfast. Remember, head down, shoulders slumped, and pretend you have had the worst night of sex in your life," he says and winks at me with a smug smile as he walks out of the door. I glance down at my thighs and grimace when I notice the bruises on the inside of my thighs from last night. Matched with the scabbed and scarring wounds on my arse and my toenail that is now black from where I fucked it up a couple of weeks ago, I sure do look worse for wear. But I trust in Luca. If he says he has a plan, then I believe him. I have to because what else do I have?

Once we are ready and out the door with my freshly braided hair and slight limp to my step, we head towards the breakfast area. At least in a place like this, I don't have to worry about people staring because all the women and kids are not allowed. But there are some side eyes from the men, obviously curious about how Axel's night went with his chosen one. The inner petty child in me wants to roll her eyes and flip them all the bird, but I do as Luca has told me, keeping my head down and making my way gingerly to the common area. Luca has given me a little run down while he bathes me. I have to dish up his food now and take his plate to his seat, then get my own food and sit quietly beside him. Luca sidesteps me, walking down to the end where his mother sits. He kept his eyes lowered as he spoke to another man beside him. I swallowed thickly, nerves starting to creep in severely. Surely, Luca's mother will notice it isn't Axel. I wonder if she will alert everyone or keep quiet out of fear of talking. I grab a bowl and join the line of women who are single file in cue, waiting for their turn. I glance around the line, up to the table where food is set out. It's a high, narrow timber table with a stainless steel countertop and large pots of oats, some fresh fruit, dried fruit, and milk in glass jugs. For simple people in the middle of nowhere, they sure do eat well. When I eventually reach the front, I fill the bowl with oats, pour on a small amount of milk, and scatter some dried fruit over the top. I am out of my depth. I don't even know what he likes. I take the food, place it down in front of him, and repeat the process for myself. Once I am seated beside him, I dive into my food. I feel like I finally have my appetite back and want to eat.

"Ho—" I start to ask Luca how his breakfast is, and then I seal my mouth shut, forgetting that we no longer have the freedom of speech around each other. I take another mouthful of food and pause briefly with the spoon on my lips as I feel Luca's hand on my thigh, giving it a small warning squeeze. Maybe I need a collar and leash because, sickly, my body becomes heated with his large hands on my thigh. He is my forbidden fruit. I glance around carefully, trying not to make it too obvious, and then look back down at my bowl. Only Luca and I know about our physical exchange. The air around us becomes intense and heavy with our private exchange. Luca shovels more food into his mouth with his left hand, but his right-hand moves up my thigh slightly, closer to my pussy.

Feeling desperate, I focus on my oats so I can try harder to keep a straight face. His fingers scrunch my gown fabric, and he pulls my gown higher. I can feel the cool breeze sweep across my bare thighs now, and I shiver. His large fingers rub over my intimate skin, creating soft patterns. Teasing me with every touch.

My father walks in, snapping both of our attention instantly. My gown gets dropped, and Luca glares at him tensely. I notice that Luca's grip on the spoon has tightened so much his knuckles are fluorescent white. I brace my elbows on the table, ready to get up and run at a moment's notice. Axel must have been found. But Father storms past us, with two other men tailing him. All faces wearing the same grim expression. His hand lands on a random guy's shoulder, and Luca swears under his breath. I look at him, mouthing what, but he shakes his head at me carefully, letting me know I need to stay silent.

"We have a betrayal within our family. Jackson here has been a bad boy," he says loudly. His chosen one weeps across the table, but the scorned look my father gives her cuts it off.

"I will not allow such things in our family; the bad energy needs to be rendered."

Everyone had followed one another out of the common area and through the clearing, deep into the thick of the forest. Luca told me to just go with it and follow everyone, but his words didn't make the expression on his face. He doesn't just look worried; he seems utterly heartbroken and almost sick. I want to ask him what is happening but I bite down on the tip of my tongue. We follow a path through trees, pace over a path of thick pine needles and twigs, and then we finally get here. We are in a large clearing with nothing but grass and a timber cross-like structure in the middle. Like a human wall, Jackson is brought into the middle as a circle is created around the clearing. Although he is clearly sad and regretful, he doesn't try to run. It's like he knows his fate and accepts it.

"Axel, come forward, you can help."

"Stay here, and don't make a fucking sound," he says quietly to me. Another sentence that only both of us share. I watch as he makes his way in the circle. The white clothes on him are unsettling. From the back, he looks too much like Axel. Luckily, from the front, I just have to gaze into his eyes, and I am reminded that it's not. I watch carefully. Luca and Jackson share a silent conversation with their eyes, and then Luca helps tie one wrist to the end of the timber pailing and then moves around the back of him to do the other. His face is grim. Grief-stricken. Dread settles in the pit of my stomach, and I begin to shake. Reality is settling in. This isn't just a punishment like what I have received. I guess they need the women no matter what they do. The men? If they disobey their ways, the punishment will be much, much more severe. Tears well up in my eyes.

"Today, the crows will feast, and we will all be cleansed of the lingering essence of the betrayal," he calls out loudly. Turning his head around, ensuring everyone around the circle heard his words. He pulls a short knife from behind his back in his waistband and slices up the center of Jackson's white muslin top. I jump out of my skin when I hear a crow's squawk from above me, high in the trees. I want to sink back, disappear into the shadows of the trees, and pretend this isn't happening. But my feet are also stuck firmly in place. Jackson glances around the group with his heart broken eyes falling on his chosen one. It's a silent goodbye between them both. I always thought all the men here were evil and treated the women like shit. But the emotional goodbye they share tells me something different. He was one of the good ones. One of the ones that wanted change. He must be Luca's friend, too, and right now, my heart is breaking for all of them. My dad brings his knife up and points it into the sky. Jackson's eyes crawl along everyone's faces until they find mine. He gives me a soft nod. I understand. I nod back, giving him the silent promise. The promise I will get his loved ones out of this nightmare.

"In the name of the crows and all our family lives for. I sentence you to death," My father yells as he brings the knife down and slashes it across Jackson's throat. Blood spurts out, and his head falls forward. The silence stretches out for a long time, and then it begins. The crow high above me becomes loud. I hear branches moving, and the squawk grows louder as it makes its way closer to the clearing. Luca finds his place back beside me and laces his fingers with mine. I feel his pain, and I feel his anger.

"Turn around, Birdie. Don't watch." His hushed voice tries to reason with me. But I can't stop looking at the horror. More crows start to come in, answering their buddy's call. The loud flapping of wings and endless squawks as they rustle so close to us now remind me of my nightmares. The first crow lands on his arm, tilting its head at all of us curiously, then squawks loudly, nearly piercing my ears. It moves up Jackson's still arm, tasting the blood. That is enough to send the rest of the crows into a frenzy. They all come down in a thick black fog, completely covering Jackson and fighting over him. The ruckus is loud, and it's messy. My wide, fearful eyes watch as a crows beak tugs at a soft piece of flesh from under the collar bone. Its claws are embedded in the shoulder as an anchor for support. The relentless tugging makes bile rise to my throat as my stomach turns in knots. The last straw comes when it pulls the skin free, and as it hangs loosely from the crows' dark beak, another crow comes in to try and steal it. They begin the game of tug of war, each one refusing to give up the small piece of flesh. I finally turn away then cover my face with my white sleeves while

I wonder how often Mom witnessed this exact thing before getting me out the first time.

An hour later, we leave, heading back to the village. No one says a word. They couldn't even if they wanted to, but to be fair, I don't think they would. We had to stay there until there was no chance of recognizing Jackson as crows fought over his insides. It was the most disgusting thing I have ever seen; a horror movie on TV could never compare to what I have witnessed. Violet moves close to Luca and me as we return to the clearing. As I reach out to her for comfort, Luca pulls me back.

"You can't. Go with Violet to the laundry room and take care of today's jobs, and we will talk tonight, okay?" He then leaves me standing there alone with Violet. I swallow back my ill feelings and wait until we have tonight alone to talk. I give Violet a soft smile, but the fakeness of it leaves my face feeling like it could crack and shatter into pieces at any given moment. The air flowing through the village has an invisible stench of death about it. There's the darkness I knew was there from the start, but in the depths of the cult, the true nature of it is much darker. It's evil, with the heart of the cult being made of insane, brutal men that hold some fucked up god-like complex. After giving Violet a slight nod, I start walking towards the laundry area, and she walks silently beside me. We reach the laundry room, and I can hear noises inside, indicating that the crow's feast from earlier has already been forgotten by the other women in this village. I take a small breath and then make my way into the laundry. My feet quietly pad through the building until I find a space for myself. Violet has already found her place on the other end, folding dry linen that needs to be returned to their homes. I sigh as I throw dish towels and washcloths into a large drum and start bashing it with the paddle. Blocking it out from your mind seems to be everyone else's way forward, but I can't. I stand there, eyes locked on the once clean water, now turning murky and grimy from the dirty cloths. Bile starts to bubble to the surface of my throat. I swallow rapidly, over and over, working my muscles, trying to keep it down. But it's no use. As the brown water swirls around my paddle, almost angrily, I cover my mouth with my hand and take off running outside. I fall onto all fours in the long grass to the side of the laundry room and empty the contents of my stomach. As the back of my hand presses on my lips to wipe the remains of vomit, I belch once more as I climb back up and onto my feet. I head back into the laundry room to finish the washing. In a robotic state now, I jab at the cloths, turn them in the water, and repeat the process while staring through my vacant eyes because god knows I have let my mind drift off far, far away.

The day has been a long one. Every day here is long. While I wait on our bed for Luca, I wonder if time passed quicker when I was in the pitch-black pit, alone and terrified. Or are the days passing slower in the center of the evil chaos? While sitting with my legs crossed and folded under me, I take out my braid and fluff my long hair between my fingers. I massage my scalp and appreciate the small bliss of doing what I would normally do at home in my own company. This is as relaxed as I have been since I have been here. I listen to Luca's heavy footsteps coming up the small steps and through the front door. His eyes land on me through the open doorway, and he slams the door behind him, looking relieved to see me.

"You look good waiting for me on the bed," he all but growls at me. He stalks me, ripping off his fluorescent white clothes like they burn his flesh.

"I miss seeing you in black," I murmur, watching him close the space between us. He pushes me down, a large hand nearly covering my entire chest as he holds me on the mattress. Restraining me, I look up into his smirk.

"I fucking hate wearing that shit. Trust me when I say my patience is wearing thin. I have spent years and years watching, waiting, and planning to eradicate this entire fucking cult. Now that I have you here and I have had a taste of the life we could have, I want out now." He bites my lip, cutting it, then licks the blood off of it. His hand moves up my chest and locks around my neck. He applies a soft pressure.

"Tell me, Birdie, should I burn them all to the ground now and leave with you? I could, you know. I could rip every single one of them to pieces without a second thought if it means you survive. Or should I keep being the good fucking boy and keep up this façade so we can get Violet and the other kids out? I made a promise to them a very long fucking time ago, but now you are all I crave. Knowing I could throw you on my Harley, run away leaving everything behind absolutely kills me. But then the young ones look to me like a golden knight, here to save them and I die a little more inside. I may act confident and in control with my future actions, but you better believe there is a storm inside me that becomes more and more furious. I don't know what to do!" He snaps with his chest rising then dropping, over and over. His hand, still grasp at my neck, now has his thumb drifting over the soft skin under my chin.

My lips open, and a whoosh of breath comes out as I go to speak, and then I shut my mouth again. Am I evil for wanting to see him tearing them all limb by limb? Covered in their blood while he pleasures me.

"Birdie..." My name comes from his lips as a warning growl.

"Why can't you save the kids and kill them all right now?" I ask, but my body is starting to get lost in the deadly erotic thoughts. I raise my hips slightly so it gives his knee, which is placed between my legs, a soft caress.

"If they even get a whisper that I am coming after them, they won't hesitate to hurt the kids if it will save their own arses. I can't risk it. The crows will be feasting on much more than just my best friend," he says and then nudges my pussy with his knee. Our bodies are good at reading each other's needs and wants. I raise my hips again, sliding my pussy over his hard knee, becoming breathless.

"Then we wait," I breathe and bite my own cut lip. His brooding eyes follow the movement, and he smirks.

"I will pretend to hate every moment of it, I promise," he bends his head down and suffocates my reply with his mouth that claims mine. I open my mouth to him, letting his tongue in to explore the depths of mine.

"You were a good little wife today. I should have hated it. But I really didn't," he mumbles after breaking our kiss. He presses my neck harder, flexing his fingers, and his eyes become enthralled by the sight. I rub against his knee again, and he hisses.

"Take your clothes off and lie on your stomach," he orders me as he climbs off the bed and storms out of our small bedroom. I strip off and then roll over. I wait in anticipation. Will it be pain or pleasure tonight, or both, maybe? Either way, I was up for it. The heavy emotions from today were already fading into an abyss. I keep grasping at whatever physical attention Luca can give me because it makes me feel things that aren't fear and isolation. I hear the floorboards creak as Luca enters the room again. I want to see him. I want to drink in every hard, muscled ripple on his body. But I obey and wait. His fingers wrap around my ankles, and then, bringing them together, he binds them. I try to move my ankles, but he pulls the bindings tighter in warning.

"Don't move, Birdie, or I may have to punish you," with an almost wistful tone. The bindings pinch on my skin, but I don't protest. I am confident that I can take whatever he gives me. He moves up the bed and grabs my wrists, binding them as well. Then, my wrists and ankles are pulled closer in the same direction and bound. I suck in a breath and struggle against the motion. I feel like I am being folded inside out like a pretzel. I am naked, completely bound, and left so vulnerable. I feel Luca's fingers slip down between my pussy and push deep inside. He groans when he is met with my desire. His fingers slide in and out, gliding perfectly over my slick need.

"Still so tight, Birdie. Maybe I should get the good doctor to make you a virgin for me again," he whispers.

"I'll kill you if you let that man anywhere near me."

"Maybe my death would be worth it." Soft Luca is gone, and he is back in beast mode. I can hear it in his words. I am noticing my body doesn't know the difference between fear and desire, though, because as scared as I am with the thought of the doctor coming anywhere near me, my needy muscles clench around Luca's large fingers. He starts moving his hand up my backside and spreading my juices over my rear.

"Oh," I let out a soft, surprised sound. This is something I was not prepared for. He rubs my rear opening, almost massaging it but not penetrating it. He inserts his fingers into my pussy again, stroking my clit at the same time with his thumb. Growing impatient, I want to move against his hand and seek my release. But I can't move with the bindings, so I am completely at his mercy. I get closer to climax as his rubbing on my swollen nub intensifies. I start panting into the pillow beneath my head and moan as I just get to the beautiful peak. Luca rips his fingers out of me, leaving my pussy empty and the peak I had climbed diminishing with every passing second. "Why?" I whimper out, tears threatening to come out. As I regulate my breathing once more, Luca slides his fingers into my pussy again. They move so slowly. Tears run down my cheeks as he starts the process again. His thumb finds my painfully swollen clit again and massages it in circular motions. I grow frustrated, but I can't help but succumb to the assault on my g spots, and I once more creep closer to an orgasm I so desperately desire. I try to hold it in, but a moan escapes through my lips. His fingers leave my pussy and then rub fresh juices over my arse once again. He massages softly, and then the tip of his finger penetrates my hole. He slides it out again, coating his tip in my juices that are running down my crack, and then pushes it back in. This time, he goes past his knuckle, causing a whimper to escape me. He moves it in and out carefully, breathing heavily with every movement. For a guy who said his patience was wearing thin, he sure is finding a lot of patience right now. My patience was shot, though. "Please, Luca, this is torture." I plead.

"I disagree. This is the hottest thing I have ever experienced in my life." His finger keeps up the movements, and the deeper he goes, the more pleasure I feel. This is totally different. I've never had any anal play before, and never did I think it could be this good. Luca shuffles behind me, and then I hear a slapping sound. It's loud and angry. It goes over and over. He's wanking. He pulls his finger out of my arse, slides it down under me, and finds my clit once more. He rubs it, all the while still tugging on his own cock.

"Fuck..." he groans and then smacks his stiff shaft on my arse cheek. I can feel the dampness of his pre cum, but I know it's not enough to indicate he has reached his climax yet. While still rubbing my clit he amps up the assault. I come undone and climax. I wither under him and coat his hand in my cum. My throat burns from the harsh, animal-like moan that rips from my throat. While I am still in my own world, Luca positions himself beside me. One hand wrapped around my bound ankles, pushing them further towards my head, and his other hand pushing aside one of my arse cheeks. His iron-like shaft nudges at my arse entrance.

"You're too big," I say when I realize what he wants.

"Like fuck I am," he growls and edges inside me further. A burning in my arse follows, and I bite down on the pillow.

"Try to relax, Birdie, or it will hurt more, and either way, I'm getting in." His hand that was holding my arse cheek apart slips below me, rubbing in my fresh cum. He then smooths it around my opening, and his cock, still has the tip nestled in the entrance. I breathe in and out of my nose, trying to relax while still latching on to the pillow with my teeth. He pushes in further. This time, teamed with even more lube, it slides in a bit easier. I feel sore and full at the intrusion, but it also makes me feel sexy as hell. I keep biting the pillow as he nudges more. He then slides back a bit and then forwards. Stinging follows the movements, and my eyes prick with tears. "Am I the first to claim your arse?" he asks in awe. I nod my head slightly, teeth becoming sore from gripping so harshly on the pillow.

"Good, I am the first and will be the only one," he says, sliding in and out. He doesn't go right to the base. Thank god. This seems to be enough. He slides in and out a few more times, painfully slow, leaving stinging in its wake every single time. Then he pulls out quickly, groaning, he shoots warm cum all down my arse.

I am wrapped tightly in Luca's arms, falling asleep completely fucked, in both senses of the word and content. Luca's soft snore is close to my ear and almost becomes like a lullaby, helping me sleep. With the snore now a white noise hum, sleep grabs me with both hands and pulls me into its dark embrace.

The sound of crows is loud all around me. They made a black curtain that cloaks me from everything else. "Luca!" I scream while my hands cover my lowered head as I try to keep the crows off me. "Birdie!" he calls back. I risk glancing up, but as I do, crow's feet come diving towards my eyes. "Ahhhhh!" the scream rips from my throat. I cradle my head in my hands once more. I feel cold. Am I dying? All I can see is the whirlwind of black around me, growing in thickness, and the noise from their deathly squawks so loud that it feels like my skull is cracked open. "Birdie, I can't get to you!" he screams. Tears flow down my cheeks, and ice settles all around me. Spreading over the ground and up my legs. I slap at it, trying to brush it off, but it takes hold of me. "Oh, Birdie. You have been a bad wife," the sneer snatches my attention, and I look up into the face of evil. Axel's chocolate brown eyes hold a stare full of torment, and I am left feeling unnerved.

I wake up with a large, sucked-in breath. Sitting up quickly, I grip the blankets around me. Luca sits up now he is awake.

"Birdie, are you okay? You are dripping with sweat."

"I'm so cold. Everything is freezing."

"Babe, it was a nightmare. You are safe here with me," he soothes me quietly. I lay back down and let him cradle me in his arms.

"What are we going to do with Axel? He can't just be let out."

"Was your nightmare about Axel?" he asks while tensing beside me.

"Yeah..." I mumble into his chest, trying to warm up and be as close to him as I can get. I don't care what he says about me sweating. It feels like my bones are solid ice.

"I don't like the thought of you having a nightmare about Axel," he says now, clearly letting me know how unpleased he is. I can't help but snort.

"It wasn't that kind of dream, Luca." "I don't care. I should be the one haunting you in your nightmares and the one pleasuring you in your dreams. There's no room in your life for anyone else," he grills me.

"You're crazy."

"I know. Don't ever forget it."

"What if he gets free?"

"He's my twin. We have never done life apart. But if it comes down to it, I will always choose you, Birdie. He won't ever touch you again. Anyone that tries will find themselves with missing limbs."

"I hate having to make you choose."

"Don't tell me your feelings for my dear brother are changing?"

"I didn't say that! He is death reincarnated. I don't know how you two can be so different."

"We are and we aren't. We are very similar in some ways, Birdie. Even you can see that. The darkness he has, I have it too. I just look at our cult in a completely different light to what he does. He would die for the cult's beliefs. I would die trying to save everyone from it." We lay in silence as I mulled over his words. He is right in some aspects. But my energy and body recognize the darkness Luca carries within him. Everything about Axel makes my skin crawl. I eventually fall back asleep. This time, no crows are waiting for me, and I don't have Axel waiting to haunt me. I'm groggy as I start to wake again. No light creeps through the thin lining of fabric covering the small square, wood-framed window off to the side. I lay there silently listening to the odd chirp from a bird in the distance, high up in the trees, slowly waking and letting the world know that the sun will soon be up. Luca stirs, taking a deep breath into my long strands of hair while at the same time tensing his massive arms around my small frame and pulling me further into his possessive embrace.

"What a morning delight waking up to you in my arms."

"Mmm, I can feel your delight stabbing my arse."

"My cock wants what it wants. Who am I to deny it?" he all but sighs.

"Buuut. Deny it, I will, just for this morning. Let's go check in on Brother Dearest before everyone else gets up. Then tonight, we will figure out this shit once and for all." Luca rolls away from me and climbs off the bed. I stay put and watch him get dressed into his white, flowy, linen outfit. I grimace slightly, with him catching the small movement. He gives me the same arrogant, lopsided smirk he gave me back in Coastal Town.

"I can't wait to have you wrapping your arms around me, the smell of my leathers in the air, and us riding off on my Harley. That little taste of freedom I got was my fucking entrée for the life I am going to have with you."

"I can't wait for this to be all behind us. White really washes your complexion." He snorts, holding his hand out to me. I slip my hand in his, letting his large fingers wrap entirely over mine as he hoists me off the mattress. He pulls me flush against his chest with the same smirk, still tugging at the corners of his mouth.

"In the future, I will try to remember that white is not my color." Luca let me out of his tight hold and picked up a neatly folded gown from the small chair in the corner of the room. He carefully slips it over my head, and I stay still, enjoying the softer side of him once again. My arms relax, becoming floppy, allowing him to lift them gently and push them into the sleeves. Like his real-life doll, he is caring for me, and I don't shy away from his attention.

"Let's go. It'll be light out soon," he whispers. We leave our house and make our way in the dark through the village. He ducks and weaves, and I follow suit, copying his movements, trying to be stealthy. We make our way through the damp grass that has the early morning dew set on it. The barn's outline comes into view around the back of the village. A mix of emotions fills me as we get closer to it. As we head through the double timber doors, the whole structure groans, almost as if it is unhappy that we are entering it. Luca feels around the wall and then flicks a switch. Soft lights flick on, giving us vision right down to the back of the barn.

"Won't they see the lights?"

"Nah, not these ones. There are the larger fluorescent lights I have left off. They would definitely see those," he says, pulling me along with him and refusing to let go of my hand. I swallow thickly as we walk past the room on the corner of the corridor I stayed in. The room I nearly ended my life. We walk further to the back, past empty stables that I had paid no attention to before, right to the back, where a small, plain door comes into sight. The old cupboard seems as if it would potentially hold a mop or some shovels. Not prisoners and cockroaches. I blow out a long, unstable breath, and Luca wastes no time unlocking and pulling the door open. I gasp when I take in the sight of Axel. His hands are bound behind his back, feet bound, knees bound, mouth taped shut, and a blindfold over his eyes. He is slumped against the back corner in what looks like an awkward and painful position. Luca sees my expression and then regretfully says, "Look, I had to tie him down like this, so I knew he wouldn't be able to thrash around and make noise."

"Do you think I feel bad for him? No, I'm far past that. It's unsettling seeing him again, no matter the circumstances." Luca turns back to Axel, removing the blindfold and crouches low, getting more on his level.

"I will remove this tape so you can eat and drink." Luca places down a bag he had been carrying from the house.

"If you make a noise, I will slit your fucking throat, Axel. And then I will fuck your precious Birdie on top of your dead body." When Axel nods, Luca rips off the tape, taking the two-day stubble with it. You would think I would be sanitized to the horrors after seeing crows pick apart a man's body in front of my eyes, but I still wince when I see the red spots all over his cheeks from the facial hair wax. Luca pulls out a bottle of water and gives him a drink. Axel is baby-like, suckling desperately on the water that his brother holds for him. I smile. He looks pathetic, and it makes my soul sing with fucking happiness. His eyes glance up at me as he swallows the liquid down. He sees my ecstatic smile, and as his lips pull away from the water, they turn down, letting me know how unhappy he is.

"You think you're safe with him? I could have looked after you, Birdie. Taught you the better way of living. My brother will destroy you worse than I ever could have."

"Don't worry, brother. She knows. And she wants to be with me anyway. Now I have had a taste of her. I wouldn't let her go even if she did want out, though."

"You beast! She is not yours to taste." Luca grins at him. It should unsettle me. It would be any sane person. But I'm not sane. Not anymore. He re-applies tape over his mouth and pushes Axel back farther into the black space. Axel starts making muffled noises through the tape. "She tastes fucking good, too," Luca snipes at him and then slams the door shut. He turns, facing me with furrowed brows. "Now, my little Birdie, I hope this suppresses your curiosity because this will be the last time you see him. Now get on with your chores for the day, baby." "It's still dark out. Do you think it's a little early for chores?"

"What do you suggest we do then?"

"Watch the sunrise?" I answer with a smug coating of humor. Luca crosses the space between us and pushes me against the back wall opposite the cupboard. His fingers grip my gown, bunching it in his hands, and he slides it up my legs.

"There's one thing that kills me. Something I need," he growls but is conflicted at his own words. "What? I'd do anything for you."

"I know you would, and that worries me sometimes. You deserve better than my wicked arse." I run a finger down his nose and smirk at him.

"What do you need, baby?" I throw his little nickname back at him.

"I want to whip you while you're bent over the concrete ceremony bed. He took that from me."

As I walk alongside Luca, failing to match his giant steps, so take two to his one, I chew my bottom lip and twist my long strands of hair around one of my fingers. I must appear like an innocent, doe-eyed girl following the grim reaper straight into hell, naïve and hopeless. But as much as my nerves are fraying and sanity is non-existent, part of me feels like a full-blown thrill seeker. I have watched multiple movies and read hundreds of books about sick and twisted women who fall for the villain and don't fight back. I hated every single one of those women I read about and watched.

I always screamed out loud, "You stupid bitch try and escape!" Now as I follow along like a good little girl, desperate to please Luca and stay right where I am in the middle of fucking hell, I realize I have become one of those women, and I have certainly fallen for the villain. We enter into the dark hut. I stand in one spot while Luca walks around, lighting all the long, narrow lanterns surrounding the room. As the soft flicker of lights ignites around the room, the cold, vacant slab sits in the middle, almost calling my name. I walk over to it and run my fingers over the surface. The ripple and bumps in the concrete tickle my fingers with the small vibration running through them. I can feel Luca's eyes on me. The weight of his stare is heavy. I have an internal battle of wanting to turn around and catch his delicious eyes on me and wanting to stay with my back to him so I can keep feeling his stare at my back, waiting for me. No expecting me. I want to hold some power between us, but I give in. I once again accept the fact I will obey. As I turn slowly, soft orange hues flicker over Luca's face, and a lopsided smirk appears behind it. He's drinking up every part of this. His hand snakes out, and he latches on to the bamboo stick perched on a small table. My eyes follow the movement of his fingers tensing around the stick, knuckles turning white. With a subtle tremble running through his body, he picks up the stick and then flicks the tip of it into his other hand. He smacks it firmly against his palm, over and over.

"Do you think even a sadist can be worthy of true love?" he asks me while still smacking his hand.

"I think maybe two kindred spirits can find love in ugly circumstances."

"Ugly? Yeah, I guess this fucked up life can be called ugly. But baby, seeing red welts on your arse from what I am about to do to you already has me rock hard, and I see nothing ugly in that image." I lick my lips. It's a rough swipe from how dry my lips and mouth are.

"Need me to moisten your lips with my cum baby?" I gasp, and as my chest rises, my nipples brush against the cool fabric. The fresh, crisp morning air, partnered with my arousal, makes them pucker and grow hard. I subconsciously raise my hand and rub one of them, trying to ease the feeling of pins in them. My hand drops when Luca's hungry eyes zone in.

"They look as hard as my fucking cock. Bend over the concrete, Birdie, before we run out of time." I angle myself over the concrete and lift up my gown. The wispy fabric tickles me as it floats over my bare legs. Almost like it is tricking me and setting me up for what is to come. I feel the warmth of Luca's body on my backside. The room is quiet, aside from our heavy breathing and the soft whistling of wind sneaking through the small cracks in the timber door.

"You still have a small amount of scabbing on your arse cheek, yet somehow your arse still looks like a wet dream and perfect in my eyes," Luca bites out. It sounds strangled, so I peek back over my shoulder and appreciate the strain he is under. His neck veins are raised, and his cock is pushing alarmingly hard against his white pants.

"You going to fuck me instead?" I tease him. I know I am poking the bear but walking the line of danger excites me. The feeling of danger and pain is better than the numbness and dead feeling.

"Tsk, tsk, Birdie. Don't provoke me. Now turn around," he says back to me. I face straight ahead and grind my teeth together. I know what's coming. I wonder if I will hate it as much as I did when Axel did it to me. I don't have to wonder for long. A loud crack fills the quiet void, and pain radiates from my arse cheek throughout my body. My legs weaken, and I feel my knees tremble under my new heavyweight. Liquid sticks to my thighs, and I open my eyes wide when I realize that, this time, it isn't from blood. There's a tingling in my clit, and I want more of it. I want that feeling to grow until I scream from a climax. I push my hand down under me, and between my legs, I find my clit and pinch it gently between two of my fingers. Luca whacks me again with the bamboo, and I whimper loudly. The pain is great, but the needy muscles in my pussy clench hard. I moan and rub my clit in firm, circular motions.

"Oh, the fresh red marks on your skin are like my calling card. My mark shows the fucking world I am yours, and you are mine," Luca growls, whacking me hard right across my arse again. My knees give out, and my upper body on the concrete slab is all that keeps me off the ground. My fingers are still working on my clit, the pressure building with every second that passes. Luca spreads my arse cheeks and slams his hard cock into my saturated pussy.

"Were you going to cum without me?" he asks, thrusting into me at a painful speed.

"Harder! Fuck me harder!" I yell but barely recognize my own voice. Luca grips my hips, holds me up because the lord knows my legs have gone, and he pounds into me relentlessly. "Do you want more?" he bites out.

"More! I want it harder!" I snarl back. He pounds more, balls slapping against the underside of my pussy in painful hits. The world goes blissfully white around me, and I scream out when my orgasm hits me with unimaginable force. My face and chest collapse down on the slab, and my arms going weak now, too. Luca falls over the top of me, groaning and grinding his hips against me as he fills me up with all the cum he can. Luca gently pulls his twitching cock out of me. Cum dribbles out with the motion, and he smiles, eyes raking over my behind. I pull my panties up and lower my gown before turning back to him.

"What now?" I ask in a breathless voice. I brush my long hair out of my face and wipe away the beads of sweat off my forehead.

"Now we play along again. Hopefully, only for the day."

"Okay, what? I wouldn't kill for a shower right now."

"That's on my list as well."

"List?"

"Of the places I want to take you." He rolls his eyes as if I am meant to just know these things. "You know what's at the top of my list?"

"Yeah?" he asks curiously now while he holds the door open for me. What a gentleman.

"Your motorbike..." I reply, making my way past him, and giggle when I see his shocked face.

"I think you have just made that automatically go to the top of my list, too."

"What was at the top of your list?" We walk hand in hand down the path and back into the village.

"Your bed back in Coastal. The night I laid you in your bed, and I realized you would never be made for this world, I decided then and there I wanted to fuck you in every position possible in that bed." My mood starts to sour at the memory. Remembering that Luca could have easily gone against his brother then and there, I wouldn't have had to live through these terrors. We return to the hut as resentment throws me back into an angry mood. Luca can feel my moods change and curls his fingers tightly around my jaw.

"You want to know a secret?" I glare at him and then divert my eyes so they are away from his face.

"I like you being mine to control right now. But I fell in love with you the moment you opened your take-no-shit mouth. Your strong spirit and independent soul did something to me. I got a taste of a different life. Yeah, I am fucked up. I'm completely fucking sick, and you should be running for the hills. But I was selfish back then when I wanted you here, and I'm selfish now when telling you that when this is all said and done, I won't let you go even then. But I do want the strong old Birdie back."

"The old Birdie is gone," I say quietly, fighting back the tears. Luca strokes my lips with his thumb.

"Nah, she's still in there. She's just waiting in the shadows until it's safe to come out again."

28

The day moved in a blur. My jaw ached from how often I have ground my teeth together throughout the day. Things felt different. I don't know if it is because of the words exchanged between Luca and me this morning or because the thought of home was at the forefront of my mind. But I had a fire in my belly, simmering away with my anger fueling it. My resentment and hate are like gasoline. Pacing backward and forwards across the small lounge space, back and forth. I need to get out of this place. I'm selfish and should listen to Luca and think of the children. But I can't. All I can think of is they snatched me out of my life as if it was their right and threw me into this living hell. I flick the curtain back that covers the small window in the living area. The sun is low behind the trees now, and nighttime is upon the village. I don't know what is keeping Luca, but the agitation of waiting for him fuels the fire even more. It's burning hotter, giving me the feeling I will explode. I chuckle bitterly. Yesterday, I was happy to wait for Luca. I let the curtain drop and then go back to pacing. Counting. 1,2, 3, 4 … On five, Luca bursts through the door with a gust of wind at his back and leaves blow over the ground and settle around my feet.

His face is stricken, and one word comes out of his mouth, "Run," he wheezes out of breath from running.

"Why? Luca, what's wrong?"

"Run!" he yells at me. I hear shouts in the background and a rush of activity spreading through the village. My eyes flick to Luca's, almost pleading.

"I can't leave you here."

"Axel got out. Someone found him. They know everything. They know a large portion of us are planning to get out. They want to nail all the traitors to the crows' crosses. I won't let you die like that."

"What about the kids?"

"I am going to do what I can. Follow the back road out of the village. Run as fast as you can, and don't turn back. I will send what kids I can down that way and stall everyone else."

"You will die!" My voice hitches as I suck in a distraught sob.

"Birdie, just fucking run!" he snarls. I hear voices closer now. My father's loud voice tells everyone to contain Luca and me.

"Bedroom window now. Don't fucking argue. If something happens to you, I have nothing left to try to fight for." I didn't argue this time. The thought of Luca giving up on life was motivation enough. As I push open the narrow window space, I yell over my shoulder, "I'll wait up the road for the kids." I know he heard me even though his heavy boots descend the short steps because the house is so small. I shimmy out of the window, shuffling quickly through wood panels.

As I drop to the grass, my gown gets caught on a nail that is sticking out, and a ripping sound follows. I stand and tug at my dress more so it becomes clear of the nail. My gown rips further, so there is now a slit right up my thigh. I can't dwell on my newly exposed flesh. I hear the ruckus outside our living quarters and take off running. I don't turn back. I weave through the houses, ignoring the worried stares of the grown wives just getting woken by the impending chaos. My eyes briefly lock with Jackson's newly made widow through her open door. Her eyes go from annoyance to wide fear when she sees me.

"Get up the road with the kids. Luca is going to meet us all there!" I say in a whoosh as I keep running. I see him as my superhero who will single-handedly save everyone. I sometimes forget he is purely human like the rest of us. My legs work as fast as they can, I have never been a keen runner, but I try my best to gain distance between myself and the village behind me.

Robin comes into view and she ducks behind the laundry house. A torch in her desperate grip is the only light that gives me a hint as to her whereabouts. I grab her elbow and tug her towards the road.

"Luca said to go this way." I say desperately. I'm thankful to see she is one of the ones that are part of this rebellion, although I had always suspected from past comments.

"I have to try to get the van. Although I don't know how to drive it," she hesitates with eyes flicking around. Yelling is loud behind us and I force myself not to look back.

"I can drive! I will come with you." I blurt the new idea at her with eager eyes. Finally something I can help with.

"No sister. If Luca sent you this way then follow his orders. If he sees you still amongst the chaos he will lose focus. He loves you Birdie.

He has a real love for you that all of us could only ever dream of. You need to do what he says so he isn't distracted. Go," she urges and keeps creeping behind the laundry house through the overgrown grass.

I throw my hands onto the top of my head and grip strands of hair in my balled fists while I view where Robin is headed and towards where the road should be, in the pitch black. My fathers voice booms closer to me, making up my mind.

"We will find every single traitor and the punishment will be death!" he grumbles as I hear another house get broken into followed by screams. I take over towards the darkness once more.

Looking around for the beginning of a main road, I become confused for a moment. Everything is the same now it's dark. Small paths, big roads, and endless amounts of tall pine trees all seem the same. I stand at the back of the village, swinging my head from side to side. I squint as hard as possible as if it will help give me night vision to see clearer in the dark. I jog towards an area that looks clear and squint my eyes again, desperate to try to see anything at all. I see the makings of what looks like a road. I take off down it as echoes erupt, bouncing off the trees around me. My toes smash against rocks and stray sticks, but I keep forcing myself forward and pumping my legs as fast as they can go. My cheeks become flushed, and my heart rate is working over time, causing my chest to become tight. "Come on, Birdie!" I give myself a small pep talk. I run so far that the soft ambient lights from the torches and homes disappear, leaving me in nothing but the black night. I grow wary and hug myself securely. How did Luca think I would get the whole way out without light? I remember we came through a gate when I was in the back of the van, so I continue jogging, hoping I would come to it soon. I lift my arms and put them out in front of me, pushing them into the open space and hoping it will help me avoid kissing the trunk of a tree painfully. My burning lungs force my now slow jog to a fast walk. I wheeze loudly and grill myself, thinking I should have worked on some fitness back home. A flicker of a small torch shines through the trees, reflecting off the round trunks. I shy away from the light, ducking down, unsure whether they are friends or foes.

"Birdie?" A whisper comes from that direction. It must be Luca. He's the only one that knew I was coming down this way.

"Yeah, I am here," I climb up and brush the pine needles off my knees. Luca walks closer to me with nothing but the circular torchlight between us. As the torchlight flashes over the road, I sigh in relief. The soft gravel and dirt track let me know that I am, in fact, on the main road.

"I was worried I was running in the wrong direction," I say. Luca walks out from the tree line, crosses the road, and stops before me.

"We need to go back," he says. But his voice is different. I turn my head toward the winding road into the darkness to where I had just come from.

"Why would we go back? I'm nearly out."

"We just need to," he says, gripping me around my elbow and tugging me back toward the village. His hands feel softer, and he doesn't have the leathery calluses I am accustomed to. My eyes travel up his body, realizing his entire frame is smaller. My eyes reach his face and land on his eyes. The eyes staring back at me are a solid chocolate brown. There are no beautiful soft highlights in them. I try to pull my arm out of his grasp, but he squeezes his fingers tighter. "You're not Luca!" I say frantically.

"Luca is gone. The crows will be waking up to him laid out as their breakfast. Now let's try this again, my chosen one. The doctor will fix up your misgivings again, and you will be sealed as mine once and for all. Your mouth is getting taken care of, too, because I am done trying to be Mr Nice Guy!" He drags me along the road painfully. My feet scrape against the stones as I try to dig them deeper, like magic brakes. Mr Nice Guy? He and I are not even on the same planet, not even in the same fucking universe. He is delusional.

"You are a fucking psycho. Let me go," I argue with him. Luca can't be gone. He's mine, and I am his. Forever.

"Kill me now," I plead. Axel stops and pulls me up close to his face.

"So you can be with Luca in death? I don't think so. My brother won't win. I won't let him," he seethes, spit flicking over my face.

"I won't live without him," I sob, still trying to tug at my arm.

"Wanna know what, Birdie? Maybe you watching him become bird feed will be a good way to get over this obsession with him."

We walk for so long. It was quicker for me to head the other way because I was running. This time around, it was becoming the road that never fucking ends. The road that is taking me once again to the nightmare. I feel chilled from the fear of seeing Luca's dead body. Finally, a soft scatter of lights comes into view, and dread overwhelms me. I start pulling at my arm again, desperate to escape. I see a figure running from the distance towards us, causing Axel to come to an abrupt halt. As the figure gets closer, I see that it is my father.

"Here comes Luca's killer now. Did you know it was daddy dearest? I watched him stab Luca and the life leave his eyes." Bile rises in my mouth, and I swallow thickly, pushing the vomit back down. I hug myself, scared of what is about to become of me. My father reaches us and looks over my face with a mixture of anger and sorrow. Mother Fucker. I will kill him. I glare back at him, hoping all my thoughts are portrayed on my face. My father grips Axel's shoulder and pulls him in close, whispering something in his ear. Axel's body goes tense as the whispering continues. Axel starts pulling me toward the tree line, away from the village.

"Where are we going?"

"Just taking a little detour, Birdie." My head snaps back to my father, who is standing in the middle of the road, holding his torch. His world is crumbling around him. The entire cult his father's father created. Their family legacy. My family legacy, I guess. That is the positive I will cling to right now. My head turns back to Axel who is ripping me through shrubs and weaving us around tall pine trees. I kick the back of his knees. He lets go of my elbow for just long enough that I jump out of his grip. Axel stands back up straight and stares me down. I step away from him slowly, but he matches my movements. We do this over and over, both eyes trained on one another's, each one of us refusing to back down but also refusing to make the first move of pouncing or running. Axel's hands are tense at his sides, fingers splayed open, ready to be able to grab hold of me at any moment. Everything changes in an instant. Axel takes another step toward me, and his eyes widen with shock. A deep wheeze comes from his body, and I see a large, tall figure over his shoulder.

"I'm sorry, Brother," Luca's pained voice murmurs close to his ear.

"Why?" Axel wheezes louder.

"I'm saving your soul, bro. Forgive me," Luca says, then drops Axel to the ground before him as he takes his final breath. My hands cover my mouth, and bravely I glance up at Luca. Tears roll down his cheeks while he shakes his head back and forth in despair. I run to Luca, wrapping my arms around him.

"You are alive," relief washes over me. Luca's breathing is ragged, and he struggles to breathe. I feel the wetness coating the front of my gown, and I know it. I know what it is. I don't want to see, but I need to. I pull back slightly to view down between us. I can see the slight red color, but it's so dark. I let go completely, bend down, grab Axel's torch, and then shine the light on Luca's torso. Gasping loudly, I see the amount of blood on him and the deep wound at the center of his stomach. Luca's pale, barely able to stand.

"I had to make sure you were safe," he says before he collapses to his knees.

No, no, no. I drop to the ground beside him and press my hands on his wound firmly.

"Don't you fucking die on me, Luca!" I scream. Shuffling sounds and the snapping of twigs follow my screams. My father's figure makes his way from behind a tree and takes in the sight before him.

"What a waste. I never thought it would be my child that would ruin us," he sneers, growing more and more wild as he takes in Axel's dead body.

"You were both going to save the cult's future," he continues. An idea comes to me as he finishes his sentence, and desperation is all I have at this moment in time.

"Save him, and I'll do whatever you want."

Father bounces his eyes between me and Luca's near-dead body.

"I promise I will be the perfect chosen one. I will never go against you. You can have your cult. Just save him."

"I won't let you and Luca be together."

"I know. I will be with anyone you choose as long as he lives." My fingers, now coated with blood, press harder into his wound.

"He's running out of time, and so are you!" I scream at the top of my lungs.

He runs a hand through his hair and sighs.

"You were chosen for Axel; it's not that simple." I scoff at him angrily.

"Like fuck! This isn't about creating perfect bloodlines and believing in a higher power. This is about men controlling women and having a god-like complex when you get to choose who breeds with whom. I'm not stupid. But I will follow along as long as you save him!" He crouches low and squats on the ground, looking over Luca and me.

"Fine, we will try and save him. Then he goes far away."

"Deal." My father pulls a walkie-talkie radio out of his waistband and calls for help.

"Bring the van down and bring the doc. I'm waiting on the main road," he says, not taking his eyes off me. He stands tall again and starts walking out of the trees and back to the road. He sneers over his shoulder, "I mean it, Birdie. This is the deal you make. If I ever think you are double-crossing me again, Luca will be dead for good this time."

I nod vaguely at him. My brain is in a spin, but all I know is that Luca has to survive. I can't imagine a world without him in it. I wanted to go home so badly. I was running towards home only thirty minutes ago. Now, as I assess Luca's dying, lifeless body, I know for certain he is my home. If he breathes, I breathe; if he is here, so am I. If he ever gets free, then I will, too. I shake my head at the last thought. I know deep down that I had just signed that reality away. Commotion starts through the trees and goes to where the road is. I can hear deep voices in heavy conversations, and then before long, there is a flash of torch lights, and then there is my father, the doctor, and some other men I remember from the ceremony.

I get protective of Luca. Seeing them coming in and outnumbering us, I grow panicked. I glare at all their faces and climb over Luca's body to be positioned before him.

"Birdie, you must let us near him if you want him to make it through this."

I sigh. He's right, so I scuttle to the side. My back smacks against a tree trunk, making bark to jab me through the gown. I watch everyone work to lift an end of Luca each. He is larger than all of them, so it's no easy feat. I dig my fingers into the earth beside me and scrunch pine needles and soil in my hands. They start slowly struggling through the trees, all puffing already from the heavy work.

"Birdie, follow us," Father yells over his shoulder with clenched teeth.

He's an old man probably struggling to get out of bed on cold, frosty mornings. Watching him struggle with Luca, knowing that it is to save his life, leaves me grinning ear to ear. I follow quietly behind them. Smiling at their backs, I tell myself this is payback enough... for now. I climb into the back of the van once Luca's body is placed on the van floor. This is the same van I arrived in. It smells old with the rusty typical motor vehicle smell that lets everyone know it is outdated and created before you were born. My father and the doctor sit in the back with us, talking in hushed voices and starting to cut off his clothing. The trunk gets slammed behind us, so we are closed in. The two other middle aged males walk around the van, climb into the driver's and passenger's sides, start the van, and pump the gas when it groans, desperately struggling to come to life. I push myself into the corner, as far away as I can manage, and hug my knees. My hair slips down around my legs like a safety blanket, shielding my eyes from the gash in my gown. The road is bumpy, and I wait. I count to 100 very slowly, and then the wheels crunch over more gravel underneath me. We have arrived back in the village. The van door is pulled open and raised up high. There is now a larger group of men waiting. One grabs Luca's feet and pulls at him roughly. This angers me, causing me to lash out. A growl almost escapes me as I slide across the van floor and boot the male in the chest, causing him to stumble backward and let go of Luca's feet. My father is right behind me and grips the back of my arms. We are so close, and it feels much too intimate with us both sitting so close on the ground of the van.

"Birdie, the deal only extends so far. Don't push me. Daughter or not. I will let him die and just force you to breed with the men here." His evil, retched breath covers my neck. A shiver runs up my spine, and I grimace. I snatch my arms from his grasp and slide out of the van.

"Just make sure he survives," I bite out and move away from the van.

"Ah, Birdie?" My father calls after me.

"What?" I ask as I stop and take in the havoc before me. There were bodies and blood on pathways, huts on fire, and children and women grouped in the center of the village, surrounded by men with guns.

"You are back in the barn until I can trust you." My father calls after me. I hear grunts and banging, so I know they are taking Luca now. A man starts at my back, holding a hunting rifle, and I chew the inside of my cheek. Never in a million years did I think I would ever think this, but I want to return to the barn. I need to separate myself from the chaos here for a moment. How had everything gone to shit so badly?

Like nothing had happened, we have returned to the old routine. Violet brings me food, then leaves quietly. I am ecstatic to see her. Knowing she has survived. I wanted to ask who else had made it. Did they know she was part of the rebellion? Did all the children and women make it? I knew what the answer would likely be from the mutilated bodies I saw, but the morbid part of me hoped they were the bodies of the bad men. Violet's beautiful small face now has a deep, dark purple bruise around one of her eyes, and she is even more reclusive than before. Just as Luca had hope for their safety and well-being and had future plans to get them out, they are now diminished and nothing but a distant memory.

My father hasn't been in to see me. Hell, I don't even know if Luca is still alive. It was on the seventh day that my daily routine had changed. My father comes in, the old deadbolt alerting me to my new company like every other visit. I sit on the cot waiting. My legs are crossed, and my new gown, which Violet left me, gives me much needed privacy. My father's presence is overbearing; he knows he holds all the power over me now. His arms are crossed at his old chest, and gray peppered hair frames his wrinkled face. I stare at him, waiting.

"Luca lives, just. He lost a lot of blood, so he needed transfusions and a lot of sutures. But he lives, and when he is well enough to walk on his own, he will be banished."

"Does he know about the deal I made?" I ask. My father's stern face grows more serious and disapproving.

"Does it matter?"

"I guess not."

"Are you going to behave, Birdie, or do we need to revisit the hut in the meadow again?"

"I'll behave," I say quietly. The fucked in the head part of me is wondering who would spank me this time now the twins won't be around.

"We have found another male for you, Carter. Because this goes against anything we have dealt with before, we will hold a ceremony tonight. It will be a gathering with the loyal men and women, so they can see you are willing. It will also help settle everyone's nerves." Carter is the name of my new fated male? Interesting.

"Why are you still pretending all this higher power shit exists when you know that I know it's a power trip and croc of shit," His gray eyes grow wild, with his brows joining together at the center of his forehead. He drops his arms and clenches them at his side.

"I'll also make sure the doctor stitches your mouth shut tonight. Can't have you spilling any secrets, can we, Birdie."

I stutter, shocked. "Y-you can't be serious?"

"I am. And he will. Tonight will be a great ceremony, and even better, I won't have to listen to your smart mouth the entire time. Enjoy your day, *Daughter*," he draws out the daughter and smirks at me openly before he locks the door and leaves me in the room. My fingers run over my lips, backward and forwards. I can't have my mouth stitched shut. He has to be bluffing. I tell myself that over and over. Willing for it to be true. The day doesn't fly by. It drags painfully slowly. I sit in the same spot on the cot, scratching my head and brushing my fingers through my hair. Fidgeting nonstop to keep myself from going stir-crazy. I keep licking my lips, sedating their dryness, and also shuddering, thinking that it may be the last time I ever get to lick my lips. Hours have passed when I hear footsteps thudding against the dirt floor. A younger male opens the door, sauntering into my room like he owns everyone and everything before he stops directly in front of me. His grass-green eyes bore into mine, and striking black hair gets tossed from his face with one shake of his head. He crouches low so we are level with each other.

"I haven't had the pleasure of meeting you yet, Birdie. Now that I can see your beauty for myself, I am highly pissed I haven't met you sooner." His low, growl-like voice states matter of fact close to my face. His breath smells of peppermint, like he has just brushed his teeth. This doesn't surprise me because when he flashes me a toothy and just as cocky smirk, I get a good look at his perfect white teeth.

"Has flattery not been able to land you a wife yet? Poor you, have to settle with me."

His loud bark of laughter bounces off the walls around us.

"I have heard you have a mouth on you, but it's better than I thought. The lips that match the brass words are just as enticing." He stands straight and holds a hand out to me. I slip my hand in his and let him pull me up, so I'm standing. I was so lost in getting irritated with him that I got angry at myself for accepting his hand so easily. My eyes crawl over his body. He is tall like Luca but slimmer.

"And," he carries on, touching my chin with his long finger, "As for a chosen one... I preferred to not have one. Call me special. I am their hunter and like to do my own thing."

"This place is fucking confusing. I thought strict routines and fucking ceremonies were part of the gag here."

"Yeah, to keep everyone in line. But when you're in the inner circle, you can do whatever the fuck you want," he shrugs as if we are discussing the weather.

"Inner circle? Jesus Christ, lord, have mercy on my fucking soul. Another sicko ready to rape me."

"Nah, won't be no rape happening, Birdie. I won't touch you until you beg me for it," he says, arrogant and so sure of himself.

"That will never happen. If you're in the inner circle, you know why I am here. You know I am here just to save Luca's life. Nothing more. And how can you be so blasé about living your life of freedom while innocent people get fed to crows?"

"I didn't say it made sense, Little Bird. And as for Mr Muscles, yeah, I know about that," he grinds out. He is still holding my hand and gives it a little squeeze.

"I asked to be paired with you. When I heard about everything that had gone down. I got back from my hunting trip and decided the only woman I would be paired with was one that actually had some fucking life left in her. I want one with an attitude that will serve my arse to me if I deserve it. Now I am in front of you, I have realized you are that and more. So, sorry you are stuck with me because of Luca, but better believe I'm not sorry I am stuck with you!" he smirks at me, pitch-black strands of hair partly covering one of his green eyes.

"You won't get a bratty wife if my mouth is sealed shut."

Carter's eyes become hard like steel. "Trust me, that won't be happening."

"How could you ever stop them? They are evil and are a law unto themselves."

"Inner circle, remember, Birdie? I can and will do what I want. If they want venison served for dinner, otherwise I might just put a bullet in their necks instead," he shrugs off what he says; it's all in a day's work, clearly.

Carter seems cold, unattached, and uncaring whether he lives or dies. Each and every man I have met in this place has a darkness in them, yet all in a different, obscured way.

"Let's go, my soon-to-be bride. It's party time," he pulls me out of the room. I keep following behind him closely. What was it with me feeling safe around the rebellious ones living by their own rules? Somehow, I trusted this man, even though he was leading me like a man leads a lamb to the slaughter.

We stop by a large, steel tub that's connected to the side of the barn wall. It's already filled with warm soapy water.

"Here," Carter holds out a small cloth that was hanging over the side of the basin, "give yourself a wash, it might make you feel better," his soft tone takes me back a little. I snatch the cloth out of his hand. "I doubt some water and cute bubbles will help make any of this better."

As my hand submerges into the warm water, I think on this stranger beside me. I pull the cloth out, squeeze the water from it and wipe my face with it before asking, "How long are your hunting trips?"

He leans a hip on the steel tub and folds his arms over his shoulders. "Depends, I can just head out for the day, or I pack some supplies and go out for a couple of weeks. Usually before winter I have to try to bring in as much as I can so I am gone a lot more then."

"What do you hunt?"

"Anything that moves and can be eaten," He shrugs with a smirk.

"Who are your parents?"

"Dead, accident when I was younger, apparently."

"Apparently?"

"Mmmmm story is a bit dusty in details so I don't really know exactly. I choose not to think about it now."

"You don't seem to care about anyone here, why don't you leave? People wouldn't even notice if you were on a hunting trip." I submerge the cloth once more, biting my lower lip, wondering if Carter could be our way out.

As I wipe myself under my gown, his eyelids grow heavy and he watches my movements closely, as if he has x-ray vision, able to see me through my gown.

"No car, no money and I don't really like people. What's someone like me going to do on the outside?" He asks matter of fact.

"You could alert the police and help all these little kids?"

He scoffs. "I was once one of those little kids and no one came to save me. Nah I'm here minding my own business. It's not all bad. Once in a while they let me hold a wild party. There are some things you will see more of now you are with me."

I drop the cloth back into the tub and meet his eyes. He nods towards the door to indicate we need to keep moving. As we start walking, my mind is still buzzing.

"One more question?" His shoulders shake, and I hear a scoff come from him.

"I doubt that. But as you were."

"How come Luca was outcast so fiercely and had to fall in line. You and him don't seem so different." He stops in his tracks, causing me to hit his firm back.

"He was the weaker twin in the womb. But also, right from when he was young, everyone could tell he wanted out. He didn't want to be a part of this, and he was untrustworthy. I'm content with what I have and am okay with being their hunter as long as I have my freedoms. We went our way with getting our freedoms totally differently. So no, we are not the same," he says to me over his shoulder and pulls me out of the barn's large double doors. The thick stench of burning hits me hard. There is a haze in the dusk air. It makes the near-black sky almost murky.

We walk around the buildings and head towards the gathering area in the middle of the village. There is a buzz of energy. No children in sight. All adults. Well, from what I can see, there are teenagers, but here they class them as adults. Hot orange glows in the middle of the chaos. There is a large bonfire, and men wearing crow masks throw more branches on it, causing the licking flames to erupt and sparks to fly up into the sky.

"What is this?" I mumble. Every man has a large crow's head, and women have masquerade-style feathered eye masks. They are dancing.

This is different from what I have ever experienced here. The women are singing and giggling.

"This is my fucking wedding. Done the right way."

"No, seriously? The women—are they the inner circle who also want to be here?"

"Yeah, I guess so. The ones that clearly were running aren't around anymore." We get amongst the gathering, and I swallow hard, growing more and more nervous. Carter feels my tension and pulls me under his arm.

"It'll be okay," he whispers against my ear. My father comes over to us. I know it's him, even behind his stupid crow's head. It's always the biggest of them all, and his old, frail body gets lost in the ocean of other bodies. I gasp when my sister, Robin, steps from behind my father. She doesn't wear a mask, but my eyes are drawn to her lips. They are stitched together. The brutal-looking holes are an angry red. It wasn't even done with care. I grow angry. My fire is more wild than the bonfire beside me.

"What the fuck have you done to my sister?" I cry out with clenched fists at my side.

"This will be your punishment. You're lucky it wasn't worse. My daughters have deceived us, so this is your punishment. If you were anyone else, you would be crow's shit in the treetops right now!" he all but spits at me.

I wheeze in a big breath and cover my mouth.

"You can't be fucking serious?" I sob. "You're fucking evil."

"There will always be more people happy to be in this life. Six months on the road, and my men will have a whole new following created."

"I hate you!"

"I hope you enjoy that because that will be the last time you say that." Holding a small bag, he grins at me as the doctor comes near. I try to step back, but Carter holds me firmly in place. "No! I would prefer her pretty mouth to stay open." Carter says. My father narrows his gaze, which looks more evil with his beady eyes on us through the crow's head.

"She has other holes you can use!" he grinds out.

"I like her smart mouth. Keeps me entertained." My father runs a hand roughly through his aged hair while a mixture of a grumble and sigh leave his mouth.

"You need to find a way to keep her quiet in front of people," he says, turning on his heels and stalking away. But not before yelling over his shoulder, "What the fuck is it with my fucking kid and men undermining me over her!"

I am pretty certain the doctor said something along the lines of being like my crazy mother. But I can't be certain. My father stands up on the deck, running along the main eating area, and looks out at the loud crowd. He holds up his cup to everyone, and everyone else does the same. A new rush of fear of the unknown has me cemented in place. A strong shiver runs through my body, chilling my bones as I take in the sight of long white gowns, waterfall sleeves flapping in the wind and obedient, waiting eyes trained on father.

"We are here celebrating new opportunities, new family ties that we will be seeking and accepting into our family, which means fresh bloodlines. Something we have long discussed. We also celebrate Carter finding a pairing of his satisfaction. Have a drink for Carter," he calls out. Everyone yells in congratulations and takes a large drink.

There are moot hoots, and then all eyes turn on us. Carter takes a gauntlet-style cup from a passerby and holds it between us.

"I take you as my chosen one. Do you accept it?" he asks. I am silent. *I don't accept it. I accept none of this.* I want to see Luca. What if everyone is lying to me, and he died? I don't want to take another breath if he isn't taking breaths. With all the thoughts racing through my mind, my heart shattering for Luca, and a part of me telling me I shouldn't give up the fight, the words out of my mouth are the opposite.

"I accept," I say, taking the gauntlet from his hand and taking a large drink, completely finishing the contents. Whatever it is, I hope it takes me far away from this fucking reality.

To say I regret my earlier actions is a complete understatement. After drinking the entire contents of the drink and standing awkwardly with Carter while a copious amount of tall crow's heads congratulate us, things just got weird. I asked Carter if the drink was alcoholic, to which he giggled and just shook his head no. He is still beside me, protectively sipping away on his drink. The sky around us is completely dark aside from the bright blaze in the middle. The heat from the flames is warming my body, and I think drinking helps with that as well. My brain goes fuzzy like a fog is rolling in and settling in for the night, suffocating my ability to think for myself. I watch as two younger women sit on each of my father's knees while he is seated on a large timber chair, looking over everyone. He lets the girls sip from his cup before he takes more for himself. One of his hands is rubbing up and down one of the women's backs, and it gives me the ick, yet I'm so fascinated I struggle to peel my eyes away. When my father roughly wraps one woman's hair around his fist, my eyes stray slightly and drop to the scene in front of me. There are two men with their crow heads securely in place fucking an end each on a curvy woman that has her gown pulled right up so her breasts are even hanging out the bottom of it. The man at her rear is railing her with such force I can hear the slapping sound over the laughter and singing around us. The man kneeling in front of her face is fucking her mouth roughly. But she isn't trying to get away; she acts like she loves it. A flash of fiery ginger hair catches my eye on the opposite side of the bonfire. Robin and Wren's mother is laid out on the grass, with her legs spread, rubbing herself as she takes in the erotic scenes around her. A woman comes over to us, eyes on me, and tries to get close with her hands out, aiming for my breasts. Carter hits her hands away.

"No, she is mine and mine alone. Find another vagina to fucking eat," he growls.

"Why was she doing that? I'm not a lesbian."

"Probably because you are asking for it by playing with your pussy, and when you're on this shit," he holds up the gauntlet, "You will be anything as long as it eases your body's cravings!"

As my eyes travel down my body and catch my actions, I pull my hand out. I feel so embarrassed, so mortified. I had hitched my gown up and was rubbing my swollen clit while watching the porn show in front of me.

"Don't worry, little bird. The first time can be a bit much. But just let your body go with it. Although, trust me when I say that the only person filling your holes tonight will be me." He thrust his thumb out to his own chest.

"I don't want to fuck anyone. Take me back to the barn."

"Can't, sorry. And as I said, you will beg me for it. I will try to be a humble winner when that happens." His cocky face is all I can focus on. Loud moans and slapping of body parts are growing around us. As my heart thumps heavily in my chest, that soon gets drowned out, too. My body is craving Carters. Hell, my body craves anything that will make it feel good right now. I can feel beads of sweat on my forehead, like I have just gone on heat. My nipples ache, the pain increasing with my brain telling me they won't stop hurting unless Carter gets his mouth around them. Soft pants come from my lips. I feel like I could combust right here. I lick my lips and say weakly,

"I love Luca." It sounds pathetic. I feel like a cheating traitor. Carter runs his fingers lightly over my nipples, causing a whimper to leave my lips. My heart aches for Luca, but my body is set on one thing and one thing only. Warm juices coat my thighs, and heavy pants leave me. I need Carter in me and I need it now. As if triumphant and on the verge of gloating, he whispers against my damp, sweaty skin, "Do you want to go back to the barn, wife? I will go back to my house and be done with our celebrations tonight." He says the wife part in a taunting voice. Humor coats the word. I grimace at my pained breasts, Carter's fingers still rubbing the tips of my hard nipples. My chest rises and drops with my heavy pants.

"I-" I shut my mouth. Am I really going to do this? I rub my thighs together, squeezing my clit as much as I can. He raises an eyebrow to me in question. Fuck he is sexy.

"I want to go to your house," I say in a whoosh of breath. I'm going to start fucking his leg soon. He grabs me around my waist, which sends a sharp jolt through my body. I don't know if I will make it to his room.

"Let's go, little bird. Before you decide to sit on someone else's face," he groans. He propels me forward. But not before I catch a glimpse at his manhood forcing its way through his pants. My eyes widen. It's long! I don't know if it's as thick as Luca's, but it is definitely longer. A small wet patch is right on the tip of the light-colored material. My mouth becomes dry. God, I want that. I want to taste his excitement in my own mouth. What a waste it is on his pants. He leads me behind the doctor's clinic. The opposite side to the other houses and laundry room I have been in. We come to a small cabin, and he forces the door open and pushes me inside. The room smells like it has been closed up for a long time. It's a studio-style home. The bed is in the one and only room with a small kitchenette off to the side. There's a door at the back that I assume houses a small bathroom. His bed is basic, with no headboard, one pillow, and a woolen throw. He tosses me on the bed, rips his shirt over his head, and stares down at me.

"Take your gown off now. I want to see all of you," he orders. I don't argue. I sit up, pull the gown over my head, and then toss it across the room. I gaze into his beautiful green eyes and picture them staring up at me while I am sitting on his face, as he suggested earlier. I fist both my breasts in my hands and squeeze painfully. This feeling is becoming too much. Sweat trickles down my temple and drops down onto my bare shoulder.

"Please," I cry.

"Please, what?"

The door smashes open, and a cold gust of wind rushes over my body and licks at my wet thighs and burning breasts.

"Yeah, please what, wife?" Luca stands in the doorway, holding a hunting rifle. He flicks off the safety and aims it at Carter. Terror fills me, but Carter, the unhinged hunter, doesn't seem to care.

"Fuck off, Luca, go back to bed," he mumbles, waving his hands.

Carter then drops his hand, pushes it into his pants, and strokes his cock while looking over my naked body. The heat is still there. Lord, what the fuck is wrong with me. I am scared but still desperately wanting the orgasm my body seeks. "I'm not leaving without Birdie." He snarls then glares back at me, frowning.

"You were going to forget me so quickly, my lover?" His words send a shiver up my spine. He is back in his black combat-style pants and has a small dressing over his torso by his belly button. He's back to dressing like the Luca I had fallen for at the start. I guess now Axel is dead, so he doesn't need to pretend.

"I am sorry. I don't know what's wrong with me. But it hurts," I whimper as a cold, icy wind rushes through the small cabin and whips my puckered nipples again.

"She has had the drink," Carter says with a smirk. Luca cusses under his breath.

"I'll just tie her up until it passes. Or satisfy her myself. You're not fucking touching her." Luca growls at Carter, stepping closer with the gun.

I sob, feeling almost sick. Both their heads swivel my way. They couldn't be any more different. Luca has light brown hair with high-lights and pretty hazel eyes, while Carter's hair is like midnight, with deep green eyes that match the forest around us.

"I want you both," I say quietly. My body is fucked.

Luca curses and brushes his hand through his hair.

"Birdie, I need to get you out of here. You will regret this in the morning. It's the fucking drink Carter likes to serve at his parties."

"What's in the drink?"

"Who knows, probably some fucked up mushrooms he finds in the bush. I have never wanted to know. And I have never taken the drink." He says, like he is disappointed in me.

"I didn't know. I am sorry,"

"Were you really going to live happily ever after with this guy?" He asks, throwing his thumb in Carter's direction with the gun snug against his shoulder and in a tight grip with his other hand. "I did it to save you!" I cry out, then slip my hand between my legs and pinch my clit.

"This hurts. I'm so hot; make it stop, please," I beg them both. Carter moves to his small kitchenette and pulls a bottle from his fridge, tossing it to Luca. He catches it mid-air in one of his large hands.

"You have to be fucking kidding me. You're not touching her."

I cry when he says it. I want them both. My pleading eyes land on Luca.

"She's not going to feel satisfied unless she gets us both. It's her first time on the drink. She can't control it at all."

"You are pretty much fucking drugging her!" Luca growls.

"Just make it end!" I whimper and slide my fingers over my clit slowly. Luca stares at Carter with pure hatred.

"Just like being drunk off alcohol this would pass through her by the morning."

"Yeah but look at those sweet pleading eyes. How can anyone say no to her?" Carter says the lust filled words while not taking his steaming eyes from my body.

"Ah, shit. Birdie, I would walk through fucking hell for you. And right now, knowing you want another man to touch you is fucking hell!" He says before opening the bottle and downing the contents of the drink.

Carter grins and crawls onto the bed. "Time to taste you, my wife," Carter says, appreciating the view he has between my legs as he rips them open.

"She's my wife."

"She's our wife," Carter corrects and grips my thighs. Luca raises the gun to Carter, making my eyes go wide. Tears run down my cheeks. Sorrow? Regret? Or disappointed that my slutty vagina won't have them both.

"Tsk tsk, Luca, kill me, then how are you going to be able to satisfy every part of her body all at once?" he says, smirking at me and not bothering to look back at Luca. I pant when the sentence leaves his mouth. The image of both of them satisfying my entire body is too much. I cum hard. My needy muscles clench as I fall back on the bed, crying out loudly. It rocks my entire body, my back arching as the quiver wracks through my body. But it doesn't sedate me. I wipe the sweat away from my head.

"More. I want more!"

"You just climaxed without us even touching you. You will be getting more, our little wife." Carter says. The drink is starting to work on Luca because he slams the door behind him and works his pants off. I watch his erection spring out, and the veining monster staring at me steals my attention.

"I have missed it so much," I say in complete awe.

"Birdie, you are fucking killing me here," He grumbles but moves on the bed so he is kneeling beside me. "But Birdie? It has fucking missed you too!"

As I lay with my head flush against the mattress, Carter takes long, painfully slow licks up my thigh. He cleans every bit of my pleasure off my bare skin. His tongue leaves burning streaks on me, like his tongue is made of fire. I feel like an animal right now because I can't get enough. Nothing he does takes this feeling away. I want to be on them. I want them on me. I want them to be in me, and I want to be in them. My throat burns as another whimper leaves my throat. Luca runs his large hands down my stomach and dips it between my sensitive lips. He finds my swollen clit and starts rubbing it while Carter cleans up the last of my thighs. Luca leans down and takes a breast into his mouth. He nips at it roughly and then groans when I gasp at the sensation.

"That nice Birdie? You like it rough, don't you? What if I decide to make love to you as punishment for touching another man?" He growls before taking my other breast into his mouth and biting the end of that nipple. He moves his hand away from my pussy and brings it up to my breast to start massaging softly. I swear in anger and lash out, grabbing a fistful of hair.

"Don't make love to me."

"That's what you should get when you have been bad, Birdie. Me making soft, soft love to you." "No, please don't." He grabs my breast roughly and squeezes it, and a cry leaves my mouth from the pleasurable pain.

"You're lucky I'm not in the mood for making love," he growls and then suffocates me with his mouth as it claims my own. Carter sends a scorching long lick to my pussy.

"You taste so fucking sweet, yet you are far from it, aren't you, Wife?" he says against my pussy so his warm breath blows against it. He pushes a finger inside my pussy, sliding it in and out. "Are you sweet?" He asks.

"No!" I pant loudly.

"Do you want us to treat you sweetly?" Luca chimes in after breaking our intoxicating kiss. "No, please, lord, no." Carter slides his finger out and sucks on it. Luca turns around on the bed so his head is at the foot of the bed and then lies on his back.

"Sit on my face. I need to taste you!" I do as he orders and perch myself on him carefully. Luca grips my thighs and rips me down to him as if starving. Carter moves off the bed and stands by Luca's head so his hard cock takes up my entire view. He thrusts his hips forward savagely.

"Take it all, Birdie." He groans. Pre cum is already trickling off the tip. I grab the base of his cock roughly, and as I am about to take it into my mouth, I moan from Luca teasing my clit between his teeth. Sweat runs between my breasts and drops down onto his forehead. I swallow thickly and then take Carter's cock into my mouth. He groans and moves his hands to the back of my head, fisting my hair painfully in his hands. He pulls my head back roughly and then forces his entire cock back into my mouth. I gag as it hits the back of my throat, but he keeps going. He pushes further until he is satisfied and then pulls my head back again. He repeats the process over and over, fucking my face with intense need. I want to moan and cry out as Luca dives deeper into my pussy with his tongue, but it comes out as a strangled gag. I can taste Carter's salty pre cum in the back of my throat. It tastes like heaven. I can feel myself building up to orgasm again while my body is like a hot furnace that doesn't seem to have any chance of finding relief any time soon.

"Fuck!" Carter roars as he slams my head onto his cock again and cums down the back of my throat. Gagging sounds come from me as I try to swallow it all down and climax at the same time. I almost cry on Carter's cock. I want everything Carter gives me without wasting a drop, but I need to release the built-up sounds in my throat. I rub my pussy against Luca's face harder, getting the last of the climax out, and suck Carter's cock head with force, making sure not a single drop was wasted. I want more. This isn't enough. I am about to demand more when Luca throws me on the bed.

"Get on your hands and knees and suck my dick," He groans. His throbbing cock is desperate, angry, and red, and I want all of it. I get on my hands and knees and move to the foot of the bed where Luca is now standing. I latch onto his cock and run my teeth softly over his stretched foreskin.

"Oh, now you are just teasing me, baby," he smirks, leans forwards and slaps my arse. Carter moves onto the bed and shuffles behind me.

"These scars on your arse are fucking beautiful wife,"

"I know," Luca agrees with him. Carter pushes his cock into my entrance and then slides it deep. I suck Luca's cock deep like it is my pacifier. His hands grip me under my chin and around my throat. I look up at him through my eyelashes as my eyes water. I breathe through my nose as much as I can, but as he squeezes my throat harder, it becomes harder to breathe. Carter smashes in and out of me while rubbing my arse entrance with his thumb.

"You sure about that?" he groans to Luca, asking about him gripping my throat, but the pleasure he is feeling is too much.

"She loves it. Don't you, naughty girl?" His calling me a naughty girl while squeezing my throat has me in a chokehold. I clench my muscles, feeling the blood rush straight to my pussy. Carter hisses and thrusts into me harder.

"Oh yeah, I can feel how much she likes it." I keep moving my mouth over Luca's cock. Feeling the throbbing veins pulsate against my tongue and the roof of my mouth. Every now and then, I catch his thick size on my teeth, but he groans even more when I do that. The sick pain mixed with our sex is what we share the most. I taste Luca's salty pleasure, and I suck harder. Working my mouth backward and forwards, taking the entire length and massaging the shaft with my tongue as it's in my mouth, he cums moments later. His hands are still on my throat, and his fingers flex against my skin as he curses loudly and rocks his hips slightly while my tongue milks the last of his cum. He lets go of my throat, and my entire body has a blanket of sweat over it. My throat feels like it has been attacked with razor blades, but I want more. I look at Luca, feeling confused, while Carter is still pounding into me from behind. Luca drops down in a squat in front of me. His dick is still like steel.

"You want both of us filling your holes at the same time, baby?" He asks seriously.

"Yeah, This feeling of being unsatisfied won't go away." I cry. My body is hot, and I swipe at my forehead. Luca stands tall again and nods to Carter before Carter pulls his long cock out of me. There is a shiny film covering Luca's body, which catches the lights. His abs are highlighted, with soft, small shadows underneath each dip. I kneel on the bed in the middle; Carter grips me from behind and pulls me against his body. His own perspiration from his chest rubs against my back, and his hard length rubs up in between my arse cheeks. I snake my hand around the back of me and grab onto his arse cheek, then claw it, leaving a red trail of nail marks. My hand makes its way around to the front of him and grips his cock, tugging at it with a firm grip. His hands trail up my arms like soft butterflies, but each gentle touch scorches my skin. I start panting again and lean my head back against his bare shoulder. I never want this to end. I rub my arse up and down so Carter's erection glides up and down my crack. He pulls my hair back away from my neck and starts sucking on my neck. Luca is in front of me in the next moment, kneeling in front of me. Two very different men sandwiching me in, both as intoxicating as each other. Luca rubs the front of my pussy, while he takes my mouth with his. His tongue snakes out and rubs against my own. Carter is still sucking and kissing the nape of my neck. We are so close, sharing each other like our lives depended on it.

"You want us both in you, wife?" Carter breathes against the back of my neck.

"Yeah," I whimper into Luca's perfect mouth. Luca pulls back and lays down on the bed once more. His cock, pointing straight up with heavy balls, tight underneath. I need him, all of him, and I need Carter, too.

"Get on," Luca orders. I straddle Luca with my thighs on either side of his. I ease myself onto his cock slowly and quietly moan when I take his full length. Carter moves behind me so he is between Luca's legs, too.

"Ride him," Carter tells me. I plant both my palms on Luca's chest and stare into his eyes as I slide up his shaft and then drop back down onto it. He groans and pinches both my nipples. I rock my hips forward and ride his cock with steady movements. Carter grips my hips from behind but doesn't control my movements. He just rests his hands on either side of my hips as I make my own rhythm. I move over and over like an addict would, desperately trying to get a fix. It's not enough. I need more. Carter squeezes my hips and holds me still mid-stride.

"Lean forward, wife," he growls. I do as I am told, desperate for them to help me take away this feeling. Luca wraps his arms around me and bites my lip, and then I feel Carter's fingers swipe under me, coating his fingers in my cum. His fingers take all my juices, and I look into Luca's face when I realize Carter is rubbing it off his balls. Luca smirks at me, arrogant as ever. Carter rubs all my wetness up into my arse crack and over my opening. He pushes a finger in that is saturated and rubs it in and around the entrance. After removing his finger, he nudges my entrance with his hard cock.

"Do it. I need it," I sound like a feral animal. My throat is so sore, and my voice is harsh and raspy. Carter pushes into me. He isn't gentle, but I don't want him to be. I know I can take him. I want all of him and Luca. Carter goes right to his base so his hips are flush against my arse cheeks. I can feel Luca's heavy balls under me and Carters on top, pressing against him and my pussy. Carter lifts his leg so he is stable on his foot and the other leg balanced on his knee. Carter holds my hips still, and Luca's embrace around my back is solid. They have me at their mercy. Carter starts first, sliding out of me and then pushing back in. Luca holds me still as he pulls out of me a little and then slams his cock back into me again. They both create a rampant rhythm and fuck me together at the same time. I feel completely full, and I know it should be uncomfortable, but it feels glorious. My body is singing to me and humming with a new energy. All my g spots are getting satisfied at the same time. They keep going, thrusting, groaning, and balls slapping me and each other. It is primal and masculine. The room smells of sex, sweat, and copious amounts of cum. They push harder, causing me to cry out.

"I want it harder. Harder, and I am going to cum!" They both ramp up their assault. It sends me over the edge. I get swept away in the biggest orgasm I have ever had. A scream rips from my raw throat alongside my muscles, clenching and spasming over and over. Luca and Carter both groan and say various cuss words as they push deep inside me, reaching their own climaxes. I can feel their throbbing cocks deep within me, and I sigh. This is exactly what I needed. Carter pulls out of me slowly, and I grimace. He climbs off the bed, breathing heavily. "Anyone is welcome to join me in the shower," he offers with a shit-eating grin and that knowing smile of being right that I begged for what he gave me. He left Luca and I on the bed. I feel broken. I don't think I can move. My body finally feels satisfied. Luca rolls me over with him still in me. I can feel cum coming out of me and cringe. Luca is still as hard as steel. He smiles down at me before dipping his head and nuzzling my neck. He nibbles the bottom of my ear lobe and then kisses my forehead.

"I should be selfish and fuck you some more. My cock wants you again. It will never get enough of you, and neither will I. But you look completely fucked—pun intended—and in dire need of some rest." He pulls out of me and rolls onto his side, pulling me tight against his body.

My mind is slow and groggy, but one thing beams at me like a flash of light through the thick fog. Luca may be moody, single worded and damn right hateful towards everyone around him when he needs to be and in the throws of passion we may have unique tastes. But in a split second, that always changes and he treats me like a fragile piece of glass that may shatter at the slightest touch. When it comes down to it, he puts me first every single time. An unconditional love so strong it hurts knowing I probably broke his heart tonight letting someone else be with me.

"We will shower in the morning. I love you, Birdie." He breathes against my hair.

"I love you too, Luca."

I wake with two sets of arms wrapped around me. One set large and smelling of sweat and sex. The other is thinner but hard and chiseled and smells of lavender soap. This should be awkward, like the next day when you wake up hungover and do the walk of shame back to your house. But I felt so safe and comfortable. It didn't last, though. It never does in this demonic place. A banging sounds at the door. All three of us sit up and stare at the plain timber door. "Carter, open up!" It is my father's voice. Luca shuffles off the bed and pulls his pants on. "Yeah, alright, I am coming." He yells out towards the door and rolls out of bed, too. I'm in the middle, naked, sore, and alone. I pull the blanket up to my chin, staring at the door.

"Fucking hell can't even have a sleep-in after my wedding day before I go back into the bush," he sneers as he brushes his black hair back and out of his face, then winks at me. Luca lets out a sound that is almost a growl.

"Yeah, yeah, I know. She was yours first." He says and heads towards the door. He stands there with his hand over the handle as Luca slips into the small bathroom. Carter swings the door open. My father is standing on the top step, and I wonder if he was about to try to bust the door down.

"Luca's gone missing. Is he here?" My father asks, getting straight to the point. His hands are behind his back as he waits for his answers.

"Why would he be here?"

"Because I know how possessive he is over my dear Birdie," he says. A snort leaves me when he calls me his dear Birdie. He's got some nerve, the sick bastard.

"What are your plans with Luca?" Carter asks casually as he studies his nails while he leans against the door frame.

"Is that any concern to you?"

"If it concerns Birdie, then it concerns me, and she is rather attached to Luca," Carter says, standing up to my father. My stomach twists as I grow anxious for Carter's bravery, and my heart flutters at his kindness towards me. My father narrows his gaze and crosses his arms over his chest.

"This alliance we have between us only goes so far. We can always find another hunter. Don't forget that," My father bites out before he turns to walk away. Carter slams the door, seething with anger.

"How can such a wanker create such a beauty like your wife?" He asks, causing me to blush slightly. Luca steps out, crosses the room, crawls onto the bed, and throws one of his hefty arms around me.

"Carter, don't get any ideas. She is only mine..."

"Minor details," Carter waves his hand dismissively, causing a laugh to escape me. I quickly cover my mouth when I realize I have fucked up. Luca's arm around me pulls me closer to his shoulder so I am being squeezed.

"Birdie..." He warns me. I look up to him, side-eye Carter, and then my eyes flick back to Luca once more. Now, the next day, awkwardness is starting. Do we talk about this? Or just pretend it didn't happen? Luca breaks the silence.

"We can't stay here. I can't be here, and I won't go without her," he kisses the top of my head before continuing.

"I want to get the others out too."

Carter sighs, crosses his arms, and leans back against the closed door.

"Okay, I don't know how you can leave with a large group of people. Everyone's on high alert from the last stunt you pulled."

"Yeah, well, I think the longer they stay, the worse their torture will be. Her dad's not done with them yet. Not by a long shot. He wants to ensure an example is well and truly made of them." "Yeah, you are right. Tonight, we get them all out?"

"Agreed. Tonight." Luca says, back to being a man of few words.

"Come join me in the shower. Before I have to let you go play wifey for the fucking day."

He jumps off the bed and goes to the bathroom, completely ignoring Carter.

"I will be right there!" I call after him. I gingerly climb off the bed with the blanket wrapped around me tightly. I feel shy now.

After what we did last night, that seems pathetic, but I can't control my mind any more than I could control my body last night. I stand by the bed and tentatively slide my eyes to Carter. His green, brooding eyes are trained on me. There is no cocky smirk tugging at his lips in this moment. He pushes off the door and stalks towards me with his hands clenched at his sides. He grips me at the nape of my neck and pulls me toward him.

"I don't want to let you go. I want to take you into my forest, where you can live with me, and I can taste every part of your body for the rest of my days. But I will be a nice cunt and let you go." He pulls my hair away from my neck, and his eyes appreciate the suck marks covering my neck.

"At least my mark will stay with you for a little while after you leave. Don't forget me, little bird," he says quietly and full of anguish. He leans in and kisses me softly on the lips, then walks out the door.

"Meet me in the serving room for breakfast, wife," he says.

He is back to being cocky and humorous. But I have seen a glimpse under that façade he shows off to everyone around him. I sigh before turning my head towards the bathroom. Steam is floating out of the door. A small smile plays on my lips. I head into the bathroom and raise an eyebrow at the shower.

"We are in the middle of fucking nowhere, what do you expect? At least this lucky bastard gets a shower," he grunts. I drop the blanket and walk into the small makeshift shower. A basic metal shower head is set in the wall with a hole cut into the timber floorboard to let the water out. That's it. I climb into the steaming shower with him, and he instantly wraps his arms around me. "We have a lot to catch up on, Birdie. But I feel we are pushed for time."

"Yeah, you are right on both accounts," I grumble.

"Are you very sore?" He says while watching the water run down my legs. I follow his eyes and step back, shocked. Blood is tinting the water.

"Yeah, a bit sore. What's the blood from?" I ask. Although I'm not stupid, and I already know, I don't know why I asked out loud.

"Well, we were not gentle last night. That was definitely a night I would never have expected and a night that won't be repeated. I can't handle sharing you, no matter how hot that was," He gives me a small smile.

"Yeah, I know. I feel like I have been put through an Ironman or something."

Half an hour later, I am in a fresh gown and walking slowly to the shared eating room. I fall in line politely, gathering a plate of food for Carter and another for myself. I sit next to Carter quietly and hold my breath as the pressure of the seat causes pain to radiate through my backside. This is too familiar, yet so far from when I sat in this spot with Luca. However, one thing remains the same: holding secrets and betrayals close to the vest and hoping we make it out of this alive. I sneak the opportunity to glance around, taking in the fact so many seats are now empty. Many children are sitting quietly with their fathers, but their mothers are nowhere to be found. My sister sits further up the table, mouth still sewn shut. The string is loose enough to allow for a straw. I watch her struggle to push the straw between her lips and suck back some hot broth. Frowning down into my bowl of oats, I push it around with my spoon, feeling heartbroken. This is bullshit. They can't win. My father clears his throat loudly, making everyone's attention focus directly on him. He bangs his cup down on the long timber table to emphasize the importance of what he is about to say.

"As you all know, we have had traitors amongst us. Some that would try to destroy what we have and all we believe in. Today, we will gather in the clearing and make a great sacrifice to the crows. Our biggest yet. I welcome anyone who feels their soul and heart are no longer with us, our large family, to make the ultimate sacrifice and give yourself to the crows." My father's eyes trail along the table, eyeing every single pair of eyes. His eyes slide from Carter to me and linger on mine, boring into mine with hostility. Whatever father-daughter love he may have held once is long gone. He wants my death; it is written all over his face. He no longer tries to hide his hatred of me. I have tried to kill myself before, and maybe he thinks I will give my life to his cause today. I let my lips morph from dismay to a fuck you smirk. He scowls deeper and then goes back to being the almighty and all-knowing leader of this god-forsaken cult.

"Everyone get up, it's time," He announces. I stand as Carter stands, and he gives me a grief-ridden stare. He's never gone against the cult; he has always ignored what he does to live his own life as much as possible. But even this is too far. I can see in the look he gives me that he is struggling with his conscience. Violet and my sister walk out along with everyone else. I walk side by side with Carter, watching them closely. As we make our way back through the village towards the crow clearing, I am reminded of Luca's best friend being picked up. The memory of flying pieces of skin and his hair dropping down onto his bare torso makes my throat sting with fresh bile. I cover my mouth with the back of my hand and swallow back my belch. Carter puts his hand on the small of my back.

"You okay?" He whispers.

"Is anything about this ever okay?" I counteract. He nods tightly, accepting what I say. His mouth sets in a thin, serious line. His black strands of hair cover parts of his eyes, and I sigh. I'm not made for this life. I can't follow along. Luca said long ago I don't have a submissive bone in my body. I can't keep going like this, pretending to be okay with any of this just so I can't live. Actually, this can't be called living. Breathing? Yeah, that's as far as it would go if I stayed here like this. My future is bleak: a silent girl who only breathes until old and frail.

We make our way to the clearing, and I see women lined up on crosses. Tears slip down my cheeks as I recognize some of their faces. Every woman that had ever shown me kindness. I take in each and every one of their faces. I quickly sigh with relief when I notice Violet isn't here. But if she isn't here, then where the fuck is she? The women who bathed me, showing me a kindness no one else dared, quietly cry while their binds hold them in place. I can't let them die alone. We make a large circle, once again, exactly like last time. When I step forward, my father steps into the circle, about to start his speech. Heads swing my way, and I hear Carter cuss behind me.

"Get back, Birdie," he growls and tries to grab my hand. I rip it away so it's out of his reach. The wind picks up in the clearing, and my hair gets blown around. I swipe it out of my face so I can look directly at my father.

"I will die with them. I will not be gutless and watch them die in front of me when I feel exactly the same way as they do!" I cry out. The women gasp and look at one another. I slightly turn, looking at the row of crosses.

"Don't feel sad for me. Someone once told me I was never made for a life like this. I have accepted my decision." Two men grab me, and my legs go weak, giving out under me. I want to be strong and brave, but my body is going into shock. I can feel the blood leaving my cheeks and replaced with a cold, visible sweat. My body starts trembling like a weightless leaf in a storm. The men push me against a bare cross roughly, causing my back to slam against the timber.

"Stop! She is my wife! I have a say in what she does. Get her off the cross." Carter yells, stepping forward at the same time. His fearful eyes drill into mine while he clenches his hands into tight balls on either side of him. My breathing comes in short, fast bursts. My cheeks puff up and then deflate with every breath I try to suck in. I'm not brave. I want people to see me as brave, but at this moment, I am terrified. I won't change my mind, but it doesn't take away the fact I will probably piss my pants any moment. I stare into Carter's eyes, wishing things could be different. I wish I had had the chance to thank him for being my second protector in this place; that made me feel safe. My father pulls out his knife, ignoring Carter's words. He walks to the end of the line of crosses, closer to the circle's edge. He raises the knife, ready to drop it down over the first neck.

"The crows will take this great sacrifice today and bless us with an abundance of—" His words are cut off. His neck makes a loud crunch and whips to the side at a painful looking angle. His eyes go wide and then vacant. I look up to see Luca standing behind him, face full of fury. He lets go of my father's dead head, leaving his body to crumple to the ground. He grabs a gun from someone standing behind him and throws it across the clearing. Carter catches the rifle in one hand and, in a fast, fluid motion, flips it over and points it at one of the men who had pushed me onto the cross and started tying me up. Luca grabs another rifle from the man behind him and points it at the edge of the circle.

"Firstly, I told you she's my fucking wife, and secondly," his thunderous eyes bore into mine. "I told you if you ever try to kill yourself again, I would lock you up!"

34

People start to back away, out of the clearing. The circle slowly disperses. No one knows what to do. My father's body lies lifeless. Call me morbid, but if I wasn't half tied to a cross right now, I may dance on his dead body. A middle-aged man with buzz-cut brown hair looks directly at me. His hands are on one of my wrists with rope hanging loosely over them. His crystal blue eyes freak me out. I can almost see the thoughts buzzing behind those eyes. He's not going to give up; he isn't the type. His hand slips behind his back, and he pulls out a small silver revolver. He holds it up and trains it directly against my temple. His other hand pulls me away from the cross and holds me against his body for protection. Carter and Luca step forward, rifles now pointing at him.

"Let her go, Gregory!" Carter sneers.

"I don't fucking think so. Let me go, or she dies," he snarls.

"She will die by your hands even if we let you go," Luca says matter of fact. I feel a push at my back, causing me to stumble slightly. A loud smacking noise behind me gets repeated violently. Gregory drops the gun away from my temple and tries to turn around. A pained groan escapes him, and he stumbles back, letting me go at the same time. I jump away from him. My sisters are both standing together, staring down at Gregory's dying body. Robin, with her stitched mouth, is holding a bloodied knife. A teenage girl with a vengeance on her mind. Carter stretches his arm up; it trembles with the gun still in his hand. He is losing strength and dying slowly. He coughs, and blood droplets spray out. He points the gun at me and pulls back the safety.

"No!" Carter and Luca roar at the same time. Carter is closer to me and jumps in front of me, and at the same time, a deafening gunshot rings out. Three loud shots echo through the trees. Gregory drops the gun, closes his eyes, and folds over, face-planting on the ground. Blood covers his back. I look around. Everyone is still standing, so I let out a sigh of relief. Luca comes up behind me and pulls me into a tight embrace.

"Baby, we need to get the fuck out of here."

"That sounds like a fucking great idea. Carter, do you think you will come with us?" I ask because I know he loves living in the forest. I don't even know if he has any desire to be out in the world with the human population. I don't get a reply. Luca pulls me tighter. Carter is still standing with his back turned to me. I push myself out of Luca's arms and move around to the front of Carter.

"Birdie, you don't need to see that," Luca says from behind me. I move around, facing Carter, and let out a guttural sob. He makes a choking noise while holding his torso, which has blood pooling on his shirt and through his fingers. I put my hands over his bloody hands while looking into his eyes.

"You are not dying on me, Carter," I sob, unable to control my anguish. The pain rips through my heart and shatters my soul. Somehow, Carter manages a soft smile. Blood leaks from the corner of his mouth.

"It's worth it. I got to be the one to save you. Not Luca." He whispers, even in death, still with the same cocky arrogance before he collapses in a heap. I drop to the ground and shake his shoulders.

"Wake up, Carter!" I growl at him.

"Birdie, he's gone. We need to go!" Luca says, crouching down and wrapping his hands over my shoulders.

"The doctor could save him." I cry and heave in a long gasp. My chest hurts. This hurts.

"Even if the doctor could save him, Carter wouldn't want that. There's always a condition, and he doesn't live his life with conditions. Especially if it means you didn't get out of this shithole. Now get up, we need to go," He says against my ear. I stand then reluctantly pry my eyes away from Carter. It hurts too much to see him lifeless. Carter was so full of life and cocky humor. Luca walks across the clearing and pushes out his Harley from behind large rocks. I hear an engine in the distance, coming closer.

"Girls, go and get in the van. Everything is prepared for you both."

"What about everyone else?" Wren asks quietly with an arm wrapped around Robin

"The ones that wanted out are already squeezed in the back of the van. Go," He grumbles, leaving no more room for questions and conversation. Luca climbs onto his bike, starting it up, and it roars to life. Birds scatter through the trees at the foreign sound. I walk over to him, climb on the bike, and hug him tightly. I grimace when the vibration of the bike sends fresh pain through my backside. More tears slip down my face, and my backside is sore from Carter and Luca. The pain is bittersweet. We start slowly rolling out of the clearing. Looking back at Carter's dead body. His black hair covers his mesmerizing face, which enchanted me the instant I met him. Feeling heartbroken and torn, I wonder, is it possible to love two dark and deranged men at the same time? I don't know, but I hug Luca tighter and place my head against his back. The bike revs harder and takes off up the long gravel road. Leaving hell behind with my rock and soul mate is a dream I started to believe I would never have. I don't dare glance back again, or it may just shatter this perfect dream. The thick trees on either side of us keep going and going. After getting to the gate I came through months ago, we wind down further and out onto the open road. Wind blasts through me, causing a shiver to shake my entire body.

"Sorry, it was a last-minute escape plan!" Luca yells over his shoulder when he feels me shivering against his back.

"The freezing cold and open air never felt so good!" I yell back. He nods, twists the throttle, and roars down the road faster. I start counting. It's all I can think of to not beg Luca to take us back to Carter. 1, 2, 3, 4, 5, I keep going into the thousands until my mind shuts down and my eyes close. Sleep pulls me into its comforting embrace, giving me a break from the torment. Not just from Carter. From it all. I'm not brave enough to look in front of us until the bike starts slowing down. With one hand still firmly around Luca's waist, I use my other to hold my unruly wind-blown hair out of my face. I know this scenery. It is the road into Coastal Town.

"I don't know if this is the right place to come." I urge Luca, leaning further over his shoulder. I'm nervous about my hometown being just ahead, but I can't look away. We fly past the Welcome to Coastal Town sign. Heads turn our way as we zip through the main road and pull up in front of my mom's house. It is exactly like I left it like nothing is amiss. I climb off the bike when Luca shuts it off. He watches my face closely as I stand there dumbfounded.

"I don't know how I should feel right now. Happy? Sad? Angry? I'm so confused." I sob.

"Then confused is what you should feel," he says quietly, brushing the hair away from my face and tucking it neatly behind my ears. His hands grip either side of my face, light brown hair tickling his forehead. He's a goddamn wet dream.

"When I left you for those weeks. It killed me. I was sent back here to clean up your life and come up with a story so everyone would stop asking around for you and drawing attention to your disappearance. But I knew I would get you out one day. I would get them all out. So, instead, while I was here, I set this house up as a safe house. There are bags of money in there, cupboards full of canned foods, and bags of clothes to get everyone started." Both our heads turn as the cult van rolls to a stop on the side of the road. The driver climbs out, drops onto the road, walks around to the back of the truck, and opens it up. Everyone climbs out.

I count 15 in total. The equal amount of sadness and excitement is scary. There should have been more. But 15 got out safely, and I try to steer my emotions towards more excitement for them. They are all embarking on a new chapter in their lives. Starting a life, they should have been given right from the start. The six women from the crosses made it into the van, some small kids. But I don't see Violet. It shatters me. If she didn't make it into the van, then where is she? Everything happened so quickly. I know Luca won't know either. The ones in the clearing closest to the van got in in a hurry as they sped away, but so many got left behind. My two sisters walk towards me tentatively. They are frightened and appear out of place. Everyone does. I take the time to really assess them more thoroughly, and tears prick my eyes. They have so many of my own features. Our father's features. I feel a jolt of unconditional love towards them and am glad we look alike. I won't let the monster that conceived us taint our bond. I have sisters. I have a family. An unconventional one. But I can't wait to spend time with them, talking about everything possible. Robin and Wren stop in front of me. I pull them both into a tight hug, and they wrap their arms around me. I pull back so I can observe Robin's face. I slowly lift my hand and gently run my fingers over the string that binds her lips together.

"We will get this off ASAP, I promise," I assure her as I drop my hand back down. She nods her head. The brown, natural fiber string is so thick and coarse that I can only imagine how painful it is.

"You were so brave today. I wish I had been as brave as you. I feel like I failed everyone by wanting to throw away my life instead of facing those monsters head-on!" My other sister speaks up and places a hand on my shoulder.

"You were brave. Because of you, we all had the courage to stand up to them in full force instead of waiting for the perfect time that never would have come. We are here because of you, Sister." she says in a soft, sweet voice. She scrunches her nose up before looking at the ground and dropping her hand from my shoulder. I get it. Talking so freely is going to take some time getting used to it. Whenever she speaks, she battles with the sentences and words coming from her lips. Luca throws an arm over my shoulder, returning my attention to him.

"Come inside. I don't like standing out here like this,"

"Okay," I agree with him. I awkwardly walk alongside him, up my small steps with his arm still protectively around my shoulder. Walking through the front door leaves a breathless gasp catching in my throat. It's exactly how I left it. Photos of Mom right by the door and the small shelf where I had thrown my keys and phone so many times before.

It is as if I had never left. I walk up the small hallway and look into my bedroom as I lean against my door frame. The bed has been made. I glance at the floor and see none of my clothes I know were there the night I was taken. Luca stands at my back, towering over me and looking over the top of my head. "One day, I would like to replace your bad memories in this room with good ones," he whispers. "Let's start by taking this fucking gown off and burning it. Burning all of them." I settle on. I look over my room one more time with a feeling of unease settling in my belly. I don't know if this place will ever feel the same to me again.

"I will call the doctor to come by and help with your lips, dear," I hear a familiar voice say from the lounge. A voice I never thought I would hear again. It has a soft lullaby in the tone like it always has. I tiptoe to the lounge and peek my head in. The lounge is packed. My house is a small one-bedroom place, and having 15, no 16, people gathered in the room makes it cramped. My eyes land on her. Standing in front of my sister, inspecting her sewn lips.

"Sandy?" My voice breaks, and a lump catches in my throat. Sandy turns around, eyes wide. She leaves my sister and paces to me, pulling me against her. She pats my hair down in a comforting way.

"Oh my Birdie. You're here. You are really here." she cries against my head. She pulls back, tears running over her wrinkled face. She sniffs in and touches my face, looking over it, studying every corner of it.

"How are you here?" She looks around me and at Luca, giving him a glare before returning her attention to me.

"He came back here about a month ago and said you were in a bad place, but he was bringing you back to me. And when you come back, you will be coming back with people needing my help. I have been waiting. Watching your place every day, hoping that that day would be the day you return." She wipes my fresh tears away with her soft fingers. Her floral perfume smells like home.

"I don't care for that large man very much. But he made good on his promise and brought you home." she sniffles again.

"He saved all of us."

"I don't know where you were; he wouldn't divulge any other details," she says, eyeing Luca over my shoulder again. She really doesn't like him.

"I knew from the first day I met Birdie that if I could trust anyone in this town to help us for Birdie's sake, it'd be you." His deep voice booms behind me. She nods at him.

"I would do anything for this girl here. Now, should I ask why some of those girls look like you, darling?" she asks, squinting her eyes at me as if it'll help get more truth from me. I smirk at her and look at the group huddled on my small couches and sitting cross legged on the floor.

"That is a very long story for another day, Sandy. For now, I reckon showers and fresh clothes are in order for everyone."

"Okay, I will hold you to that." She turns around, looking over the cult group, and speaks with a much softer, slower voice than she used on me.

"I have various-sized clothes packed in bags over here. Go through them and see if there is anything you may like to wear."

An hour later, I am on the couch holding my sister's hand as our local doctor starts the process of removing the bindings on her lips. He injects some local and rubs numbing cream over the holes as an extra attempt to make this pain-free for her. He is so gentle. A stark contrast compared to the doctor they were exposed to before. When the doctor first turned up, her eyes grew wide, and her shaking was uncontrollable. I told her to trust him and that he would help her. This will be new and scary for all of them for a long time as they transition to normal life. He lifts small scissors and snips along the string in between her lips. She breathes through her mouth and stretches her jaw. Her eyes slide to me, then she clears her throat and flicks her hair back before nodding the okay to the doctor. She's a badass. Braver than I could ever be. I look at her face with admiration as the doctor uses tweezers to carefully pull the stitches out. She's going to be okay. Out of everyone here, I can see her adjusting the quickest. I place her hand back onto her own knee, give it a small pat with my own hand, and then stand up. The jeans I am wearing feel weird. Restricting. The gown was so easy to move in, flowy. I shake my head, clearing my insane thoughts, and tug my singlet down. Luca is quiet. This isn't unlike him. But he leans his hip against the kitchen countertop, staring at me. I can see his jaw working, which lets me know his brain is ticking over. I shuffle past everyone's legs and stand in front of him.

"What's up?"

"I'm trying to be patient and be the good man you seem to think I am." *You are a good man,* my mind screams.

"Spit it out, Luca," He lets out a long sigh and smoothes his hair back over his head, away from his face.

"I'm not ready to share you with the world yet. I want you all to myself for a little longer." Relief crashes into me. Good, but I am selfish. I want to help everyone. I want to support them, but being here doesn't feel right to me right now. Maybe it never will.

"What are you thinking?"

"Wait here!" he bites out and leaves me in the kitchen. He ducks out through the lounge and moves up my small hallway. His heavy black boots thump through the house. Seeing him dressed in full black again leaves me weak at the knees. He comes back a moment later and hands me a leather jacket. I eye it.

"I stashed it here, waiting for your return. Your helmet is on the bike waiting for you. We have a list to get through, remember?" he says with one eyebrow raised, almost daring me. Well, Momma didn't raise no quitter.

"What about—" I start to say before he puts a finger over his mouth.

"Sandy has it all covered. They will be okay." I look back to the lounge and watch them all as they interact with each other. Robin is running her fingers along her lips, backwards and forwards. Sandy is kneeling in front of her, holding out some antiseptic cream for the holes in her skin. Sandy's face holds an encouraging smile while my face lights up as I watch Robin dip her finger into the cream tentatively. She smooths it over her swollen lips before thanking Sandy shyly.

"What are we waiting for then? We won't get through the list at this rate." I giggle. The sound of it almost sends me into shock.

"Oh, how I have missed that sound," Luca says, lacing his fingers in mine. He tugs me toward the front door. I look at Mom's photo as I walk through the front door and smile. *I got out, Mom, just like you did.* But the happiness and relief have a weighted shadow bearing down on it. As we walk down the path to the small town and freedom tries hard to comfort us but fails, I slip the words out of my mouth.

"Luca, I don't know if I can ever start a new chapter not knowing what has happened to Violet. I feel like I owe that sweet girl my life." We reach the bike, and he plucks my helmet off the handlebar.

"I know, it's weighing heavy on my shoulders. I have never been good at sharing my plans with anyone. I work alone and keep shit in my head."

"You think?" He gives me a grim look, for once not enjoying my sarcasm. He scratches his chin, reminding me that when we met, he had soft, clean-shaven skin. Now, he has a trim beard starting, and I dig it.

"Well... I don't have a plan yet. I don't want you going anywhere near that place again, and if I go in, I know I will be shot before I even get a word in. But I agree; I have known Violet since she was a baby, and I need to know, no matter the outcome, what happened to little Violet." Luca slips the full-face helmet over my head. He buckles it up and knocks his knuckles over the top of it gently.

"Fucking you while you wear this helmet has been added to the list," he smirks.

"Our never-ending list," I chuckle. Luca climbs on the bike and I settle in behind him.

"The list that will never ever end. I will spend every second of the rest of my life with you, and it will still never be enough. I never wanted freedom until you showed me how good freedom can fucking be. That one night we had together, drinking, being carefree, gave me a snippet into how every single moment can be between us." He says, then starts the bike. He revs it loudly, the sound filling our quiet neighborhood.

We take off through the town and back out onto the main road. As we fly past the sign that says *Thank you For Visiting Coastal Town* I lean my head against his back. Because of what we have been through, Luca is the only man that I could ever trust to show my real self to. I will follow this man anywhere. I will obey his every order. I will take every painful pleasure he stows upon me and enjoy it. Because it will always be a reminder of what darkness I have been through, what I have survived, and what I have gained.

No matter how we want to see ourselves, at the end of the day, hell is inside of us. Patterned in our DNA. We will always want to be good, make slow love all night, smile at those around us and actually mean the smile. But the truth is, we can't because even though we are physically away from the cult, the essence of it will always be living in us, feeding off our souls.

I don't know if the cult will reestablish itself even after my father's passing, and I don't know if they will try to hunt us all down for revenge. But for now, I will enjoy this moment with Luca. I will enjoy our freedom, and I will enjoy kicking his arse at the pool again. We will sit at a bar and enjoy a beer together before we spend the rest of the night exploring each other's bodies.

And if the nightmares start again and the cult comes calling for our return and bodies on the crosses, well, we will cross that bridge if we ever come to it.

The end.

Thank you for taking the time to read The Haunted Past Of Birdie. Please make sure you leave a review wherever you can, as these always help us indie authors out!

About The Author

Talia Atkins is a New Zealand born and raised author.

If not being a taxi driver for her five children you will find her with a full glass of wine in her gardens or typing away on her laptop creating her next book.

You can find Talia on the following:

Facebook

Instagram

Goodreads

Tiktok